Mad Max

Dukes of Tempest, Volume 1

Brill Harper

Published by Brill Harper, 2023.

MAD MAX

First edition. September 15, 2023.

ISBN: 979-8223999515

Written by Brill Harper.

One

Cherry Miller

I'm strolling down the sidewalk on my way to work, my nose buried deep in a book, as per my usual. I don't pay much attention to the world around me because I really don't have to. What's the point? Downtown never changes. It's stuck in a twentieth century time warp—a forgotten place in time.

Sure, the main street of Tempest, aptly named, wait for it...Main Street...is ripe with charm. Delicious aromas waft from the bakery, and a paradise of petals fills the florist's window. Tools and supplies line the shelves of the hardware store, and at the end of the street, there's an old-time theater with just one screen.

But no one would film a Hallmark movie here in Tempest anymore. Nobody even comes to Tempest anymore.

That once-grand theater? Stands silent, its velvet curtains and twinkling chandeliers nothing but a memory. In between the cozy bakery and florist and hardware store, the other once-bustling shops have been reduced to desolate facades with boarded up windows, their proprietors having long since left town in search of something more promising.

Tempest is dying slowly.

We desperately need to fill the empty shops and entice families to move back. But a group of entrenched locals seem to be dead set against progress, stuck in their ways that have caused the town to sink into a lethargic state of uninspiring mediocrity.

Lethargic state of uninspiring mediocrity is a pretty good description of my life too, come to think of it.

Romance and adventure are all I dream of, but Tempest is a place of boring sameness. Every day, I see the same faces, hear the same gossip, and pass by the same tired buildings. I am stuck in a cycle of monotony that seems to go on forever. My dreams of excitement feel too far away, like they are never meant to come true. I can't leave—my family needs me.

As I walk down Main Street, I take a moment to look wistfully at the old empty bookstore and dream of a different future. One where it is still open. And I'm in it.

It's a shame Myra Hodges had to close it down. She often gave me used books too worn to sell. Or she'd let me sit behind the counter and read new books before she shelved them. She told me she needed my review for marketing purposes, but even then I knew she was just being nice to the weird, broke kid.

Even though I'd seen store after store closing down, it was the shuttering of the bookstore that made me think things aren't going to turn around. Tempest is becoming a ghost town as more and more people leave in search of something better.

It's hard not to feel trapped here sometimes. I may never get out—but then again, maybe I'm wrong; maybe something exciting will happen one day and bring new life into this dull little place.

Yeah, right.

I was born and raised in Tempest, and I expect to die here too. I'll likely be the old, scary spinster with a house full of cats. And books.

Books have always been my refuge, saving me from the chaos of my childhood home and the cruelty of high school.

Reading is my superpower. Unless you count my ability to be completely awkward in literally any situation. In which case, the world's supervillains should definitely fear me. I am red hot with talent.

Speaking of supervillains, Chad Hamilton pops out of the barbershop in front of me and I nearly run into him. "Hey there, stranger," he says in his signature smarmy voice. "Long time no see."

God, he waggled his eyebrows at me. Who even does that?

Chad wouldn't have given me the time of day in high school unless it was to torment me. But most people our age leave town as soon as they can after graduation. Chad can't quit Tempest on account of his dad being the Mayor. Chad doesn't have any skills that don't include being the mayor's son.

I suddenly became his "type" when he ran through every other available woman in town. Like I'd suddenly forget all the names he called me in high school. All the humiliation he caused me.

I was quiet, chubby, awkward, and smarter than most of my classmates, so of course I got picked on. A lot. It didn't help that my mom ran out on us, my dad drank most of his disability checks, and we literally lived across the tracks.

I force a small smile, trying to be a bigger person, but wishing I could disappear right back into my book. Chad's been a bit too attentive lately, pouring on the charm and compliments, but I know better.

He's nothing more than a predator who only wants one thing. Besides, I know how he talks about women when they're not around.

He reaches up to tuck a strand of hair behind my ear, and I take a step back, pushing away his arm. He frowns at this rejection and crosses his arms over his chest with an indignant huff.

"What?" Chad demands dramatically. "You can't even be civil?"

Civil? Like when he stole a pair of my underwear from my gym locker and hoisted them up the flagpole in 10th grade? Kids called me "Granny Panties" for a year.

I raise an eyebrow, letting him know I don't buy his act. "Chad, you can't come on to me every time you run into me in the street. It's getting old. Just accept that I'm not interested."

"Right. Not interested. How long are you going to play hard to get with me, Cherry?"

"I'm not playing games. I simply don't want to go out with you."

He gives me his best "aw shucks" look. "I know I was a dick in high school, but I've changed. Give me a chance."

Even if that were true, and it's not, he still isn't what I need. What I dream about. He may have been all that to most of the girls in my high school, but he never revved my engine.

My dream man doesn't have to be Prince Charming. I don't want a tame hero. Give me the beast, someone dark, powerful, and commanding. Someone who can take charge of any situation and take care of me at the same time.

A man who will ravish me and make me feel alive in a way I never have before.

But there is no one in Tempest who could ever live up to my expectations. Certainly not a bully like Chad. I want a wild, passionate love.

I've been saving myself for the hero of my dreams, which is just stupid. Even if my fantasy man exists, he wouldn't be found here on the streets of this little town. All men here care about are their TV sports and their six-packs. The ones in the fridge, not on their stomach.

Unless I get out of this town, I am going to die a virgin.

I dart around Chad, eager to get away from his smug overconfident...grossness. "I'm late for work." And I am. I reluctantly stash my book in my purse and hurry across the street.

I work my ass off as a waitress at Mary's Corner, the local diner. Dad's disability check doesn't go far, so I am keeping our three-person family afloat. He's sober lately, but that's usually temporary.

As for my little brother, Adam—God bless him—he is out of control and needs someone to take the reins. That is all on me since Dad gave up on that too after my mom walked out on us.

I hang up my purse and tie on my apron. Mary, the owner and cook, hands me a cup of coffee. "Good morning, pumpkin."

"Thanks and good morning," I say gratefully, taking a drink. I look at Mary again. "Your hair! I love it."

She pats the updo. Usually, Mary scrapes it back into a very tight bun that looks uncomfortable, but I suppose is easy to keep when cooking in a hot kitchen.

"Sandy talked me into bangs and a softer look. You don't think it's ridiculous?"

I shake my head. "No. It's really nice. Sandy did a good job."

Sandy is the only hairdresser in town unless you want to go to the barber. She took over her mom's shop two years ago and has been systematically upgrading the hair trends of the older generation. She does it in small doses, so it's taking a while, but it's nice to see she finally got Mary to change a little.

Mary is a great boss and I'm lucky to have this job. She never had kids of her own, so she treats me like a bonus daughter. She and my mom had been friends, once upon a time. When my mom was a person worth knowing. Not the woman who would walk out on her two kids and veteran husband with PTSD and an alcohol problem.

Mary nudges me. "I saw you talking to Chad just now. Gossip is that you are the future First Lady of Tempest if he gets his way."

Gross. First of all, his dad is a terrible mayor, and Chad succeeding him would be even worse. I'm certainly not going to rule the town with him.

I want a man who will love me unconditionally and make me feel wanted and desired–not some power-hungry guy who thinks "I'll do" in his quest to run a dying ghost town.

"I'm not interested in Chad," I tell her firmly as I grab a stack of menus and head out into the dining area, "besides, I thought all the gossip lately has been about the mysterious buyer. Anything new on that?"

The low buzz of conversation at the diner lately has been thick with speculation about a holding company of sorts buying up the empty buildings on Main Street. Nothing has changed, so I'm not sure if it's more than just idle rumors.

"Nothing new yet," she answers.

I get to work taking down the chairs and getting ready for the breakfast crowd. Crowd might be an exaggeration. But Mary does good business, and the regulars drop in as usual. Mostly retirees.

A sudden rumble of engines roars through the street, shattering the quiet. Startled, I drop the dishrag in my hands and rush outside with Mary, joining the crowd of curious townsfolk who have come out from their shops hoping to catch a glimpse of what is going on.

Down the main street, a group of three bikers are making their presence felt as they cruise slowly down the street. I can't look away. Glimpses of the chrome on their bikes glisten in the sunlight as they rev the engines, announcing their arrival.

A chill races through me, a delicious feeling of *almost* dread that makes my heart beat fast. Tight jeans and scuffed boots hug their muscular bodies as they roar past, their leather armor gleaming with a hint of menace. I shiver, enthralled by the thrill of not knowing what might happen next. It's been so long since I didn't know what was happening next. I should be scared, but I'm excited.

So is everyone around me. It's not like we've never seen a motorcycle in town. This just feels...different.

Mary squints, her eyes narrow with suspicion. "If I didn't know better," she murmurs, her voice a mix of wonder and disbelief, "I'd swear those are the Duke brothers."

The Duke brothers? Could it be?

The mere mention of their name is enough to send the townsfolk into a tizzy. They still speak of their wild antics in hushed whispers. The Duke brothers are infamous, the kind of troublemakers that make men lock up their wives and daughters at night. I was just a kid when they left town after their mother's funeral, but even I knew who they were.

I was captivated by the idea of them, like characters from one of my beloved books. They were the pirates, rogue mercenaries, rebel anti-heroes of my stories. Most of all, I was infatuated by the idea of Max, the oldest brother. He was wild and unpredictable—an outlaw who lived life on his own terms, according to legend anyway.

The wheels in my head start to turn as I try to put two-and-two together. Could this drive-by be connected to the mysterious buyer?

But before I can attempt to determine what exactly is going on, Mary clears her throat and claps her hands together with an air of finality. "All right then. We have things on the grill."

We don't, actually. But that's okay. I get it. Back to work it is.

Back inside the diner, my thoughts keep drifting back to those three bikers—and what it could mean for Tempest.

The air smells like trouble and change.

God, I hope they come back soon.

Two

Maxwell Duke

A fter our parade through the main street of Tempest, my brothers and I are still laughing about their reactions to us while we have breakfast in Mercy, the next town over.

"If I'd have known how fun that was going to be, I'd have ridden through once a year," says Dillon, our youngest brother.

"It felt like a scene from an old cowboy movie when the villains ride through town," I admit.

"Think they still call you Mad Max?" William asks, shoveling in his chicken fried steak.

I shrug, an amused smirk tugging at my lips. The idea that everyone is still talking about us should be comical, but it's probably true. Typical small town minds.

We were nothing more than three mischievous brothers back then, but the town branded us as uncontrollable hooligans. We ran wild, mostly because that was what they expected us to do, so we did it. As we grew up, our bad boy reputations were like a magnet to the ladies, sometimes even their mamas couldn't stay away. There was a lot of sneaking out of windows or hiding in closets back then. A lot of being chased by angry men with shotguns. Once, the Sheriff kept me in a cell overnight for my own safety.

But once our mom passed away, there was nothing to keep us in Tempest. I never imagined we'd ever come back. We all succeeded just fine without the help of anyone in that dull old town. More than just succeeded. We all fucking crushed it.

My microbrewery in Los Angeles trended with the right crowd, my IPA earning a lot of national attention and a lot of money. The franchises are still doing well in cities across America.

William can build anything and became a successful contractor and movie set builder. He also worked on celebrity renovations, and for some reason, famous people like to renovate a whole hell of a lot. He was in high demand.

And Dillon served his time in the army as a mechanic, leading to a civilian job as "mechanic to the stars" after coming to live with me in L.A. once he got out of the service. They don't trust their fancy cars to just anyone.

The Duke brothers were in high demand and we got paid well for it.

It wasn't until I ran into an old schoolmate of mine that I even thought about my hometown for the first time in years. Jacob Hobbs told me that he'd been back to Tempest to move his folks out after his mom had to close her bookstore. That the town was going under, dying.

My immediate reaction? A smug sense of satisfaction. Good riddance.

That place could rot.

But then Mom's sweet face flashed in my mind. She'd always said the town was our home, that the roots we had there ran deep. I couldn't let Tempest just fade away. That would be like letting her go.

So, I scrolled through the listings of the local real estate market, my heart sinking lower when I saw all the available buildings downtown. My mom's beloved yarn store, the candy store, the bookstore, the toy store, and a couple places I thought used to be women's boutiques. Closed. Empty. Even the theater.

How many times had we been banished from that toy store, rambunctious kids too wild for their own good? Yet, I still remember the windows twinkling with the lights at Christmas while the train circled around a miniature town resembling ours. We'd press our faces to the glass, starry-eyed as we watched and dreamed about the toys inside.

What little money my brothers and I earned back then for chores or odd jobs was spent in that store. Or the candy store.

Hard to believe they were all gone. Hard to believe the mayor was still there.

So the Dukes came up with a plan. Knowing the best part would be watching all the people who thought we were nothing, who thought we would fail, realize that we saved them all when they couldn't save themselves.

Big Al's Autoshop didn't need much to reopen, so Dillon would be the first getting to work for an actual income. He had plans for adding on later, making a custom shop that people would travel the country for once they finally moved up his waiting list, making Tempest a place worth traveling to. His LA contacts already let him know they are interested.

William and I are going to start rehabbing the empty stores so we can flip them into turnkey businesses. The boutiques, the yarn store, the candy store...all are coming back to life as soon as possible. Some businesses we plan to open ourselves, others we'll lease out the space for.

And new business will hopefully bring in some more women. I might be recreating fucking Mayberry, but I still want to get laid once in a while.

I have no desire for an everlasting love. I'm not meant to be a family man. Dillon, he's the one who believes in all that true love crap. He doesn't remember our dad, though. He was too young when our old man finally lit out of our lives after causing years of heartache for Mom.

I'm perfectly content to be an uncle someday instead. But we need to bring in women under seventy for all our sakes.

"So, Thunderdome tomorrow?" William asks, a glint in his eye.

Yeah, tomorrow. "They won't know what hit them."

· · · ·

THE NEXT MORNING, I ride into town solo, parking my Harley in front of the diner, my mind full of things I need to get done.

Though the streets are mostly empty, there is one person walking down the sidewalk. She's curvy and has long dark hair that hangs past her shoulders in loose curls. All my senses go on high alert. Something about her captivates me, like a powerful magnet pulling me in closer and closer.

She is watching me with a tantalizing mix of trepidation and curiosity that sends my heart racing. Her eyes dart between the door and me.

I reach for the door handle, and my heart races as she stays put. I know I am worlds away from the gentle, small town boys she is probably used to. Burly, tattooed, and intimidating, I am like a different breed of man altogether.

Her eyes drift from me to the open door to me again. Finally, she takes a step forward, and I fight the urge to wrap my arm around her, to feel her body against me.

She pauses right next to me, looking at me with beautiful smoky gray eyes. "Hi." She smiles shyly, her voice as soft and delicate as morning mist.

Holy fuck. Just like that, I'm done for.

"Hi, yourself," I say, feeling like a teenager again. I would be happy to stand here like this forever, just looking into her eyes, feeling her near me.

What the hell has she done to me? Is she some kind of witch? Maybe some kind of angel. Maybe something in between.

I love the way she looks at me with a mixture of curiosity and what seems like desire...and a little fear. It's really hot. Maybe I'm just dreaming. I don't even know this woman.

I'm supposed to be Mad Max for fuck's sake. Not a starry-eyed kid who's never talked to a girl before. Besides, she's probably too young for me. I'd have remembered her if she had been one of my schoolmates.

Hell, we'd probably be married with a bunch of kids already if I'd known her in school.

And the thought of her, round with my baby in her belly, does something to me that I've never felt before.

Some kind of carnal instinct is rising inside me. I want to throw her over my shoulder and ride back to my hotel with her. I want to kiss her senseless and make her think of nothing but how good it feels to be touched by me. I want to make her scream, to feel her come against my body as I drive deep inside her.

But I'm getting ahead of myself. I don't even know her name.

I follow her inside the diner, my eyes glued to her gorgeous hourglass shape. She doesn't sit down. Instead, she goes past all the tables and into the kitchen, so I take a seat at the counter. I am the only customer right now. Thank fuck.

When she comes out with her hair up in a messy bun and wearing an apron around her waist, I hold back a groan. Why the hell is that hot?

I could lose myself in her all day. Her beauty makes my heart ache, my cock throb.

She comes to stand in front of me, her voice huskier now than her whispered hello a few minutes ago. "What can I get for you?"

I feel the room spin. She is perfect. A goddess sent to tempt me. But there's something else there too, something that drew me to her the minute I saw her. A calm, grounding presence that makes me yearn to be near her. To stick to her like glue.

"Coffee and a breakfast special," I say because what I really want her to get for me is naked.

"Sure," she says, her voice a bit breathless. She's as affected by me as I am by her.

As she turns and walks to the coffee maker, I let my gaze linger on her curvy hips. It's like her body was custom-made to turn me on.

What's her story? I want to know everything about her, everything that makes her...her.

I never expected to find anyone so young and pretty still living in Tempest. I definitely never expected to find the woman of my dreams in the first ten minutes of being in town. I didn't even know I had a woman of my dreams. But there she is. Rocking my world when I have so many other things to take care of.

The bell on the door rings, and two older gentlemen walk in. She greets the newcomers with a bright smile.

"Morning, Cherry," one of the men says, tipping his hat in greeting.

So her name is Cherry.

"Morning, Roy, Pop," Cherry says cheerfully. "The usual?"

I recognize the old timers, but they don't seem to notice me yet.

"Yep," Roy replies.

Pop grunts in agreement as they head over to a booth, chatting to each other about politics.

Cherry glances at me, and our eyes meet. A jolt of electricity shoots through me.

I can't wait to get her alone, the thought of her writhing beneath me and moaning my name, has me ready to explode.

But I have to be patient. I can't just rush in and make her mine when she doesn't even know me. I have to bide my time and win her over. This is important, I realize.

A little later, she brings my breakfast order, I lean in closer, wanting to feel the heat of her body close to mine. Smell her. I seriously want to smell her like I'm some kind of animal.

As she's about to head back into the kitchen, I speak up. "Wait. Can I ask you something?"

She pauses and turns to look at me. "Sure."

"What's your name?" I already heard it, but it seems like a better place to start than, "Would you like to sit on my face?"

She smiles, the corners of her lips slightly lifting. "Charity. But everyone calls me Cherry."

"Cherry," I repeat, letting her name linger on my tongue. "I'm Max. Maxwell Duke."

Her eyes widen. "Max Duke?" she asks, surprised. "The Max Duke?"

I nod. "That's right." I wonder what she's heard. That I'm nothing but trouble? "My name rings a bell, huh?"

"Yeah," she admits, her eyes darting to the kitchen.

"What have you heard?" I ask, my voice low and husky.

She blushes, her cheeks turning a deep shade of crimson. "That you're...well, that you're..."

"Dangerous?" I offer, raising an eyebrow.

She nods, her eyes still wide. Seems like maybe she wants a little danger.

I chuckle, giving her what I hope is a playful smirk. "That's true. But maybe a little danger isn't all bad."

A small smile appears on her lips, and I can't help but return it. I'm already hooked, already lost in her.

"Maybe not," she says with a shrug.

I resist the urge to reach out and touch her. I want to run my fingers over her soft skin, feel her tremble beneath my touch.

But I don't want to rush things. I want to take my time and savor every moment with her.

"I..." she hesitates, her chest rising and falling as she gathers the courage to continue. Colors flush her cheeks while her gray eyes lock with mine.

I wait patiently, silently convincing her to share whatever is on her mind.

"It's so embarrassing," she whispers. She draws in a ragged breath, her eyes shimmering with emotion. "I remember you—from before you left. I was just a little girl then. My mama... God, why am I so tongue-tied?"

She's just as enchanting when she's flustered. My heart does a little trip on itself. "Tell me."

"When I was a little girl, when I played pretend, I must have married you a dozen times in my backyard under the apple tree. When I told my mama I was going to marry Max Duke someday, she made me bite a bar of Dove soap." Her cheeks burn with embarrassment as she waves her hands, shooing away her own words. "I'm sorry. I shouldn't have told you that. I'm just really, really awkward."

This beautiful, young woman has been in love with me since she was a little girl. I wish I could say I was surprised by this, but part of me knew she was the one the minute I saw her on the sidewalk outside the diner.

And until that moment, I didn't believe in "the one."

I laugh and shake my head. "That's really sweet. Nothing to be ashamed of."

Her blush deepens, and the silence stretches out between us. I'm imagining her dressed in white all laid out on my bed like a present waiting to be unwrapped.

"I wouldn't have been good husband material back then." She makes me want to be that man she dreamed about. "And I look better in a tux now anyway."

She looks up at me with her big gray eyes, and I can't help but feel like I'm staring into the depths of her soul. "Maybe," she whispers. "But you should know I also used to marry Jacob and Edward."

"Both of them?"

She nods. "At the same time. "

"Progressive. I see I've got some stiff competition. It's a good thing I came back to Tempest, then, isn't it?"

Cherry looks up at me, her eyes bright, and I swear I can feel the electricity zapping off of us. "I suppose it is," she says softly. "Too bad I canceled my subscription to *Today's Bride Magazine.*"

Just then, the bell on the door rings, interrupting the moment. I stand up reluctantly, fishing my wallet out of my pocket. I have things to do. "I have to go, but I'll be back...soon. You might want to renew your subscription, though."

"Right," she laughs, thinking I'm joking.

She doesn't know how very serious I am.

The bell on the door jingles again, and a voice booms out, "Maxwell Duke, what the hell are you doing in my town?

Three

Cherry

The whole diner goes silent as Max slowly turns toward the door.

Mayor Hamilton strides in with an air of entitlement, his plump figure barely contained within his gray suit. His gray mustache and balding head give away his age. But he still moves like someone used to getting his way, expecting the world to bow down before him.

And it usually does. He and his cronies have held this town in a chokehold for years, running it like their own personal fiefdom.

Running it right into the ground, I think. They don't like anything new. They seem to want to keep Tempest in some kind of bubble. But all they're doing is keeping out the air our community needs to survive.

And it figures the mayor would interrupt the only real flirtation I've *ever* had. And with Maxwell Duke! My childhood crush. I'm starting to hold a real grudge against the Hamiltons.

But Max isn't intimidated by him at all. His lips curl into a smile. "Mayor Hamilton, it's been a long time."

The mayor's face hardens. "What are you doing in Tempest, Duke?"

The smile on Max's face is almost wicked. It's like he's been waiting for this moment for a long time. "The boys are back in town, Mayor."

Okay, that's a little cliché, but I'm loving the classic rock vibe of this situation. It makes the motorcycle ride through town yesterday even more on point.

The room erupts into murmurs. By room, I mean the four old men and Mary.

Hamilton takes a step closer, his eyes narrowing, a vein bulging in his forehead. "You and your brothers? We don't need your kind of trouble."

"I'm not here to cause trouble," Max declares.

Mayor Hamilton scoffs. "You think you can just come back after all this time and expect us to accept you? This town has been through enough. You're not welcome here."

"That's too bad, since my company owns half the businesses on Main Street now—a few houses too—and some surrounding land."

Max's words make the mayor wrinkle his forehead. "What now?"

"I'm saying my company bought up most of the real estate here in town," Max clarifies. "We plan to make it a desirable place to live, with tourists coming here to spend their money and appreciate all this small town charm."

Though he says small town charm is like he thinks Tempest is anything but charming.

The rumors about the holding company are true then. The fact that the Dukes are behind it makes it all even wilder. What is their plan? Revenge? Or are they really going to try to fix things? I've been hoping for change, but this seems a little more than my imagination usually conjures. And I've got a really good imagination.

Mayor Hamilton narrows his gaze, anger radiating off him in waves. "You're out to destroy Tempest?"

Max shakes his head vehemently. "We're saving it. We're providing jobs and boosting the economy–all legally. We're bringing in new businesses and revitalization. You can't stop progress, Mayor."

The mayor slams his fist on the counter, rattling the plates atop it as he glares at Max. "You're not welcome here," he growls. "Get out of town before you get run out. Again!"

Max stares at him defiantly, not backing down so easily. "I'm not going anywhere," he replies calmly, meeting the mayor's gaze with steel resolve. "And neither are my brothers." He pauses for effect before adding with finality, "We're here to stay–whether you like it or not."

The mayor's face turns a deeper red at Max's words. For years, he has held the town in his grasp, using his power to manipulate and control every aspect of it. But now, it seems his reign is coming to an end. Or at least it's being interrupted.

He glares at Max, his eyes flickering with malice. "You think you can take me down?" he sneers. "You and your brothers are nothing but a bunch of hoodlums. I don't know what laws you broke to get the money for this, but I won't let you ruin everything I've worked so hard for."

Max's expression turns cold. "We're here to make things better."

The mayor scoffs at this. "Better? You mean turn it into some kind of tourist trap, where all the locals are priced out of their own homes?"

Max shakes his head. "No, I mean making it a place where people want to live and raise their families. A place where people can work and make a decent living. A place where people don't have to rescue their aging parents and remove them from their homes."

The mayor glares at him, his eyes cold and calculating. "I don't believe you," he says, his voice low and dangerous.

Max takes a step forward, his face set with resolve. "We're here to make a difference. And we will. Whether you like it or not."

The two men stare each other down for a long moment. Finally, the mayor shakes his head and turns to leave. "We'll see about that," he mutters under his breath.

I move to stand next to Max, not really knowing what to say, but for some reason needing him to know I'm on his side. Which is crazy. The mayor could make my life more difficult than it already is.

I can't afford to get on his bad side. I've been risking enough just by turning down his son's advances.

The Duke brothers are the kind of trouble I don't need. But I have a feeling they are exactly what Tempest needs.

"Did you really buy up all the empty stores?" I ask.

"Yeah," Max replies, turning to face me. "We're going to turn this town around, Cherry. It's going to be a place where people want to live and work again."

I can see the determination in his eyes and it's almost infectious. Maybe he's right. Maybe they can make a difference here.

"Can I help?" I ask, my heart beating rapidly in anticipation.

Max gives me a look full of heat and desire. At least that is what I'm going to write in my diary tonight. If I had a diary. Which I don't because I have a younger brother.

"Oh yeah," he breathes. "You can help me plenty."

I feel a sense of hopefulness wash over me as I realize that maybe, just maybe, things are going to change for the better in this town. And I'm going to be a part of it.

Maybe I don't always have to be the chubby Miller girl, overlooked by everyone unless they feel like bullying me that day. Maybe I've been selling myself short. Maybe Tempest too.

"Let's start with the bookstore, okay? I really miss that place." I'm joking, of course. I'm sure there are bigger fish to fry for the Duke brothers.

He smiles indulgently. "You like books, huh?"

"I'm a bit of an addict if you want to know the truth." I try to play it off as a joke, but deep down there is an undercurrent of sadness I can't ignore. "A little nerdy if we're being honest.

His smile softens and he shakes his head. "I don't think you're a nerd at all."

The way he talks to me makes me feel special, like I matter. It's a feeling I haven't had in a long time. Maybe ever.

"No, I really am. But it's okay. I like being a little nerdy."

"Cherry," my boss warns. "Order up. "

"I have to go anyway," Max apologizes. "Can you meet with me later? To talk about plans for the town?"

I nod. He's totally not asking me out for a date, right? Town. Plans. Got it.

"Meet me at the bookstore at eight, okay?"

"The empty bookstore?"

"Yeah."

"Sure." Since I haven't said anything too awfully awkward in the last minute or so, I add, "I probably shouldn't wear a long, white dress, though, right?"

"It might be a little dusty in there," he jokes. "But maybe for our second date."

Oh my God. It *is* a date.

Four

Max

I light the last candle and survey the empty bookstore. I may have gone a little overboard. The space is filled with flickering candlelight, creating a warm and inviting atmosphere. Soft music plays from a nearby Bluetooth speaker, a blanket is spread out on the floor. On top of it sits a full picnic basket.

This is nothing like the dates I had in Los Angeles. I never went to more trouble than making a reservation. It could be that Cherry is the kind of woman who would prefer a night out in a fancy restaurant. I don't know her that well yet. Maybe I read her wrong.

No. I'm going with my gut on this. She stood by my side this morning, knowing my reputation, and asked to be part of my dream. She doesn't even know me, but that show of loyalty made it clear as crystal to me that she is the one I didn't even know I've been waiting for.

And a quiet night in one of her favorite places is a better beginning than an impersonal trendy restaurant or nightclub.

The door bells jingle and she steps in. "Hello?"

She's rocking a simple dress that clings to her curves like a second skin. Her sable brown hair cascades in soft and wild waves down her shoulders, begging me to grab a fistful of it.

She's turning me into a caveman.

"Hey," is about all I can manage at the moment.

Her eyes light up when she sees me, and a bright smile stretches across her face. The sight of her is like a punch to the gut, and I feel my heart flip in my chest. She's even more beautiful than I remember.

The sparkle in her eyes is mesmerizing as she takes it all in—the candles, the blanket on the floor, and the picnic basket. She's just as I had hoped–appreciative yet surprised by my romantic gesture.

I motion for her to come closer, and I take her hand in mine. It's warm and soft and fits perfectly in mine. I lead her to the blanket and we both sit down, facing each other. The candles cast a warm glow on her skin, making her look even more radiant than before.

"This is really nice."

"I'm glad you like it."

I open the picnic basket and reveal its contents: a bottle of wine, some cheese, crackers, and fruit. I pour a glass of wine for each of us, and I offer her a piece of cheese.

Her eyes explore the empty shelves. "I love this space. I always hoped someday I'd work here, but Myrna didn't need any employees by the time I was old enough to work for her. Business was already too slow. But it was my dream job, being surrounded by books, helping people find just the right story..."

Perfect. "You're in luck. It just so happens I need a bookstore manager to open this place back up."

She chokes on her wine. "Are you serious?" she asks after I pat her on the back until she stops coughing.

"I can't do it myself. I don't know anything about bookstores. And I have a lot of projects already."

"You don't know anything about me either."

Oh, but I'd like to. And I will. "I know you work for Mary, which means you're responsible because she doesn't put up with shit. I know you love books. I know you understand the people in this town. And I know you believe in what we're trying to do for Tempest because you stood by me this morning."

She blinks at me like she's waiting for the punchline. "So, you're not selling the store? You're going to keep it and you want me to work here?" she asks in disbelief.

"No, I don't want you to just work here. I want you to run it. You get to name it, stock it, and decorate it, however you like."

"Basically make all my dreams come true..." she says softly.

"I thought marrying me was your dream."

She laughs. "When I was ten, yes. Then I grew up and realized books are better than boys."

I clutch my heart. "Ouch."

We talk about specifics and where to start. Then she asks me, "So you seem to know a lot about business. What have you been doing since you left Tempest? I've always wondered."

"I know Tempest is small and backwards, but do you guys not have internet? Why didn't you Google me?"

She sits back a little, sips her wine. "I didn't want to ruin my fantasy of you. I'd built up my own stories based on romance novels and didn't want to find out you were married with ten kids. You're not, are you?"

"No. I'm single. No kids." I refill her wine glass. "But I'd like to hear more about this fantasy of yours. The one about me, not Edward and Jacob. "

She blushes in the candlelight, and I'm so gone on her I don't know what to do. "It's silly schoolgirl stuff."

"Tell me."

She drinks more wine for courage. "Well, let's see. You moved someplace fabulous like New York or Los Angeles."

"Los Angeles," I supply.

She angles her head slightly, and I find myself mirroring her movements.

"You make a ton of money and meet all the celebrities doing something you're really good at like real estate or restaurants."

"Craft beer and a franchise of breweries." I inch a little closer.

She smiles shyly but doesn't move away. "You come back to Tempest on your white steed."

"Harley."

Does she notice how close our faces are? "And you fall madly in love with me and whisk me away to your castle."

"Is a bookstore better than a castle?"

"Yes," she whispers.

My lips curl up into a grin, and I take her glass, putting it to the side. "In this fantasy of yours, am I a gallant prince who woos you gently?"

She shakes her head.

"Am I the rough and rugged pirate that takes what he wants?"

She gazes at me with desire in her eyes. "Yes," she whispers.

A shiver runs through me as I whisper against her ear, "Let's see if I can plunder your heart."

My lips capture hers in a gentle caress that rapidly grows more urgent as she responds eagerly. The taste of her is like a drug slipping through my veins, and my body aches for her touch. We break apart, panting heavily.

"You're trouble," she rasps, her voice low and needy.

"I hope you're ready for it," I growl, pulling her closer to me. Pressing my body against hers.

Our lips clash, tongues tangle. My hands greedily map her curves, roving over every sweet inch of her body and committing the feel of her to memory. Her moan echoes through me, igniting my bloodstream. I want her so desperately that I feel like I might die without her.

She's mine, I already know it. But more than that even, I'm certain that I belong to her.

I break away from the kiss, my breathing ragged. "Cherry," I whisper, my voice rough with desire. "I want you."

"I...I...need to tell you something."

Just then her cell phone rings interrupting whatever she was going to say. "I have to take it. I'm sorry. It's my little brother's ringtone."

The small device rests against her ear as she braces herself for whatever news awaits her on the other end. "Adam?" Her face pales. "What? Oh my God."

Five

Cherry

We pull up to the school on Max's Harley. There's a cop car, a graffiti-covered wall, and two boys sitting on the curb. One of them is my brother.

As we get closer to the scene, I can feel my heart sink. Adam is sitting there with his friend, hands behind their backs, and a police officer speaking sternly to them.

Deputy Fortner is unamused as he turns around to face us. He tells us that they were caught in the act of vandalizing school property and had been seen spraying graffiti on the wall behind them. His eyes narrow as he takes in Max's appearance. "Max Duke. I heard you were in town."

"Billy," Max says. "You're a cop now. Followed in your dad's footsteps after all, huh?"

I watch as Max and Deputy Fortner exchange a tense conversation, both trying to assert their dominance over the situation. Meanwhile, Adam and his friend sit there, looking small and helpless.

Deputy Fortner rattles off a list of offenses, including vandalism, destruction of school property, and resisting arrest. My heart sinks as I realize how serious this is.

I can feel tears starting to prick at my eyes as I step forward. "What happens to my brother now?"

Deputy Fortner looks at me with pity in his eyes. "Your brother and his friend will have to face the consequences of their actions. They will have to attend a hearing and pay for the damages they caused to the school property. It's a serious offense, Cherry."

I nod, understanding the severity of the situation. My brother has always been reckless, but this is a new low. I know it's not my fault, but I still feel guilty. I'm always home at night. The one time I have a date, Adam gets into trouble.

Real trouble.

Max puts a comforting arm around my shoulders. "Don't worry, we'll get through this."

I want to argue with him that it's not his problem. But it feels so nice to have his support. I've been trying to manage my little brother by myself since Mama left us. My dad has had his own struggles.

Deputy Fortner writes the tickets and releases Adam to my custody.

"I'm walking you two home. I'll come back for my bike." Max says, not leaving me any room to argue.

"Who are you?" Adam asks suspiciously, like he just realized I was with a man. A man he doesn't recognize.

"I'm your sister's friend. My name is Max. And now I'm your friend too."

Adam rolls his eyes.

"Whether you like it or not," Max adds.

Adam takes a long, hard look at Max, deciding immediately that he does not want to cross him. No surprise there. Max is the size of a mountain, towering and powerfully built. The air around him practically hums with an uncompromising expression that conveys one clear message: Don't mess with me.

We start walking home, me sandwiched between my brother and Max. Adam is angry at getting caught, I'm worried about his future, and Max seems lost in thought.

Probably wondering what the hell he's gotten into.

I don't really want Max to see where we live. The only thing I have going for me in our relationship is that he doesn't know me very well. Now that he's got a front-row seat to all my problems, there won't be any more candlelight picnics. He might even take my job offer back.

A diner waitress with a troubled family living in squalor isn't the kind of thing men are looking for. Especially men like Max. He's obviously rich if he bought half the town. He's a great businessman if he franchised his craft brewery. And he's so hot he probably had supermodels in Los Angeles lining up for a chance to go out with him. A pudgy virgin from the wrong side of the tracks will not be enough for him.

Max breaks the silence. "You know, I've been in your brother's shoes before."

I turn to him, a lump forming in my throat. Of course I know he was a kid always in trouble, too, and he turned out better than fine. My own version of heroic even. But he still has that reputation that follows him around in this town. Will Adam always be known as a hoodlum?

"I used to do stupid stuff when I was his age. Got into trouble with the law more than a few times." He chuckles wryly. "But I had someone who believed in me. Someone who didn't give up on me no matter how many times I messed up."

"Your mom?"

Max's face relaxes, his mouth pulls into a subtle smile, and his eyes crinkle. Even his posture relaxes as his shoulders lower.

"My mom was tough as nails, but she always had my back. She made my brothers and me feel that we were worth more than the trouble we were causing."

"Yeah. Great," Adam says sullenly. "I don't have a mother."

My heart cracks open. Damn her for leaving us.

"I know it's tough, Adam," Max says, placing a hand on his shoulder. "But you have a sister who loves you and will always be there for you. She won't give up on you, no matter how many times you mess up. And now you've got me. For what that's worth."

Adam looks up at him, his eyes glistening with unshed tears. "Why do you care?"

"Because I see potential in you, kid," Max says, his voice firm but gentle. "You're not just some delinquent. You're a smart kid with a lot going for you. If you pull your head out of your ass before it's too late."

Adam rolls his eyes, but he seems deep in thought.

The closer we get to the railroad tracks, the more freaked out I get. "Max, we got it from here."

Max looks around. "I plan on taking you all the way home."

"You don't have to. You've done more than enough for us tonight. We'll be fine."

"Cherry..."

"She doesn't want you to see where we live," Adam helpfully informs him. "She's embarrassed because we're poor."

"Adam!" God. "I am very capable of being awkward all on my own. I don't need your help making things weird. I got this."

Adam shrugs. "It's true. You've never brought a guy home before."

I press my fingers to my forehead. "Adam, please."

Max looks between us, a small smile playing at the corners of his lips. "I don't judge people based on their financial situation, Cherry. That's not what's important to me. We didn't have much growing up either. My mom was a single mom with three hellion boys."

Despite his words, as we approach our house, I feel a sense of shame wash over me. The paint is peeling, the grass is overgrown, and the windows are dirty.

I do my best to keep it all up, but...

Max notices the look on my face and squeezes my shoulder reassuringly.

As we enter the house, the smell of stale cigarette smoke hits us. Dad smokes outside now, but the smell is still entrenched in everything we own.

I look around the room with a stranger's eyes. Yes, everything might be outdated and dingy, but it's clean. And I make sure there's nutritious food for Adam. But the recycle bin is nearly overflowing with empties.

I want to cry. Dad's drinking again.

Adam asks, "Are you going to wake Dad up?"

I shake my head, looking at all the empty beer cans. What's the point?

I hold my head in my hands and close my eyes. I breathe deeply, fighting down the sob that rises in my throat. My shoulders shake as I try to hold back the tears.

I can't lose it yet. I still have to be Adam's only parent again.

Max squeezes my shoulder and it's enough to keep me from crumpling into a hot mess on the kitchen floor. At least for a few more minutes.

I make Adam sit down at the table. I sit across from him and fold my hands on the table and Max leans against the counter.

"What were you thinking?" I ask sternly.

He looks down at his hands, ashamed. "I don't know. It was stupid."

"Stupid doesn't even begin to cover it," I say. "Do you realize how much trouble you're in?"

"I know, I know," Adam mumbles. "I'm sorry. It won't happen again."

Max joins the conversation. "You're not the first person to make a mistake. But it's what you do after the mistake that matters. You need to take responsibility for your actions and make it right."

"How?" Adam asks.

"Well, for starters, you're going to attend that hearing and apologize for what you did. And then, you're going to work to pay off the damages you caused. It's not going to be easy, but it's the right thing to do."

The following silence is heavy. I don't know what to say next. It was easier when Adam was a little boy. Now that he's getting older, it's getting harder for us to relate to each other.

"So, Adam, what were you painting on that wall?" Max asks.

Adam looks up, surprised. "What do you mean? Just some random stuff. Why?"

Max shrugs, his eyes glinting. "Just curious," he says slowly, rubbing his hands together. "Some of it looked pretty good."

I shoot him a look. Why is he encouraging him?

"I'm a fan of street art–something about the way it stands up to those in power and makes a real statement." Max grins, the mischief in his voice clear. "It's cool, don't you think?"

I'm about to put an end to this conversation, but Adam's eyes light up, a spark of interest in his gaze. "Really? You like that stuff?"

Max nods. "Yeah, I do. But there's a time and a place for it. And it's not on someone else's property without their permission. You ever tried doing it on a legal wall?"

Adam shakes his head. "No. I didn't even know that was a thing. Nothing around here anyway."

Max grins. "There will be soon. Some of the buildings I bought need some sprucing up. I've been contracting a few artists from LA to do murals, and they're looking for local artists to collaborate with."

I can see the hope in Adam's eyes. Maybe this could be the start of something positive for him.

"It's a paying job too."

I don't know if Max just made all that up to give Adam a boost and a way to pay his fines, but either way, it's enough to make me pledge my undying love.

As if he read my thoughts, Max catches my eye. I'm flooded with the memory of what was happening on that blanket before my phone rang. The heat in my cheeks lets me know I'm blushing fire engine red.

Get it together, girl.

A quick subject change is in order." Adam's been drawing on walls since he was a toddler." I reach over the table and ruffle my little brother's hair.

He ducks out of my reach but is smiling. "You gotta admit I'm way better now."

"You are." I wished there was money for more art supplies. I try, but the best I can ever do are cheap discount store items. And he goes through them so fast. "But what you did today..."

Adam looks down at his hands again, shame washing over him once more. "I know. I messed up."

I take a deep breath, feeling the weight of the situation bearing down on me. "We'll figure it out," I say, trying to sound confident. "We always do."

"You know, Adam, you have a real talent. You just need to learn how to use it in the right way," Max continues. "You'll need to let the artists mentor you."

Adam's face lights up, but then goes dark again. "Why do you want to help me? Is it just to get my sister in your bed?"

"Adam!"

"Well, is he?"

"Absolutely not," Max says firmly, his eyes locking onto mine. "I want to help you because I believe in you, Adam. And I want to help your sister too. She deserves someone who cares about her and her family."

I can feel my heart racing, my feelings for Max intensifying by the second. But I try to push them aside and focus on the conversation at hand.

I stand up. "It's late. Adam, you need to get cleaned up. And go to bed. We'll talk more in the morning."

Once he's gone, Max turns to me, his serious expression replaced by a playful grin. "He's a handful."

"I'm sorry about what he said. He can be impulsive and rude at times. More often than not lately."

"It's alright," Max says, dismissively. "I know he's just trying to protect you. And that's a brother's job. And honestly, I don't blame him for being skeptical of me. My reputation is..."

I laugh. "You're not so bad."

Max leans in, his breath hot on my ear. "But I could be bad," he whispers. "If you want me to be."

My mind flashes back to the heat of his body against me, the taste of his lips on mine.

"I should go. It's been a long night. We've got a makeshift office at the car repair shop. Can you come by tomorrow so we can get your employment contract sorted and start the process of opening the bookstore?"

I nod, a little rebuffed at the sudden change of tone. But glad he still wants me to work for him.

He pulls out a key. "I meant to give you this earlier but got distracted."

"What is this for?"

"Front and back door of the bookstore."

"You trust me with the key already?"

"I trust you with a lot more than just my keys," he says with a wink. "But seriously, I think you're the right person for this job. And I think we could make a great team."

I grin, feeling a sense of excitement for the first time in a while. "I think so too."

I walk him to the door. As he steps outside, he turns to face me. "Sleep well, beautiful."

I feel my cheeks flush again, but I manage to respond with a smile. "You too."

He starts to go, but turns to face me once again, his eyes intense. "One more thing before I go."

"What's that?"

Max grabs my hand, pulling me toward him. Before I can even process what's happening, his lips are on mine, his hands tangling in my hair.

I melt into the kiss, feeling fireworks explode in my mind. Our tongues dance in a feverish rhythm, exploring each other's mouths as if we're trying to map out every inch of each other. My body is on fire, and I can feel the heat radiating from Max's body as he presses against me.

He breaks the kiss, his breathing ragged as he rests his forehead against mine. "I'm sorry," he whispers. "I couldn't resist."

"It's okay," I breathe back. "I didn't want you to resist."

Max pulls back, a devilish smirk appearing on his face. "Good to know. See you tomorrow, gorgeous."

I watch him leave, feeling a mixture of excitement and apprehension. This is all happening so fast, but I can't deny the chemistry between us. And now, with his offer to help Adam and my dream of opening a bookstore, it feels like everything is falling into place.

But I can't ignore the warning bells going off in my head. Max is a notorious bad boy with a questionable past. Can I trust him? Or am I setting myself up for heartbreak?

Six

Max

The auto shop office is a mess of papers, with a pervasive smell of tires and stale coffee. Dillon and I go over the contract one more time, but my mind is elsewhere. Every second feels like an eternity while waiting for Cherry to arrive.

"Well?" I ask.

"Looks alright to me. I mean, if you are basically giving this girl your business with no expectations of any kind." He looks up. "That's what you're doing, isn't it? Giving this Cherry person an entire business so you can get laid, but spelling out that getting laid isn't part of the contract?"

No. Yes.

"I don't know anything about bookstores. It's better that she has the reins," I say, ignoring the getting laid comments.

Dillon sits back on the rickety chair and plops his feet on the ancient desk. "Whatever you say. Your ass looks covered, if that's what you're asking me. I just want to know how many businesses you plan on giving away to get your dick wet. I thought we were here to turn a profit."

I snag the contract out of his hands and push his legs off the desk. "I don't need to give women entire stores to get my dick wet, asswipe. This particular woman is the perfect match for the bookstore. Now we don't have to put it on the market because we will retain ownership. And it will be profitable." I hope. "But I also want to ...date...Cherry, and I don't want her to think that dating me is a stipulation to getting the job."

"Whatever you say. She must be hot as hell. I don't recall you giving an entire store to the last model you dated."

"I'm not giving her the bookstore. I'm giving her the job of running the bookstore. She's not a model, but yes, she's..." I don't even know how to describe how hot Cherry is. Her curves, her long dark hair, those stormy gray eyes. My dick knows how to describe Cherry, and is at full mast thinking about her. I adjust my pants. "You'll see," is all I say.

I try straightening up the office before she gets here, but it's not doing much good. We should probably take over one of the shops on Main Street as our business office, instead of the office in the auto shop, but I don't want to take up space that we can sell or rent. Or turn into a store that turns a profit.

Cherry knocks on the door frame. "Your brother told me to come on back."

My heart races. She's here.

She's wearing a light summer dress that hugs her curves. Her eyes sparkle, and her mouth curls in a smile.

"You look beautiful," I say, my voice suddenly hoarse.

She looks behind her like she's checking that I'm actually talking to her. "Thank you."

She slides into the seat, and I offer her a cup of coffee, warning her that it's more like jet fuel and tastes worse.

"Thanks," she says before taking a sip, wincing at the taste. We chat for a few minutes before I give her the contract spelling out that she will be the manager of the bookstore, and that while I will retain ownership, she will have full control of the day-to-day operations.

"Well?" I ask.

"I'm trying to figure out how to discreetly pinch myself to make sure I'm not dreaming."

"I can pinch you if you like. After you sign the contract anyway."

She blushes and laughs. "I think this is a great opportunity, and I'm excited to take on the challenge."

I smile, relieved that this is going as planned. I offer her a handshake to seal the deal, but she takes my hand and turns it into a hug.

"I'm so glad you are giving me this chance," she says.

I hug her back, my arms wrapping tightly around her. The warmth of her body and the smell of her hair fills me with a strange sense of contentment. I feel like I could stay here forever, in this moment, with this woman in my arms. But then, suddenly, I'm filled with an intense desire to do more than just hug her. With every passing second, it gets harder and harder to resist the urge to kiss her neck, run my hands through her hair and explore every inch of her body. My heart races as I battle the urge to fuck Cherry right there on the spot.

I pull away first. My pants are going to be a problem today. "Any ideas on what you want to name the bookstore?" I ask, trying to distract myself from my thoughts.

She smiles, her eyes lighting up. "I've been thinking about it, but I haven't quite come up with the perfect name yet. I think I need to take a walk around the space again before I make a decision."

"That's a great idea," I say, standing up. "I'll tag along if you don't mind. We can grab lunch afterward and talk more about it."

She nods eagerly, signs the contract, and before I know it, I'm leading her out the door.

"How's your little brother today?" I ask as we walk.

"Sullen. Which is normal for Adam any day, not just the day after he's arrested for graffiti."

I nod. "Teen boy. Sullen goes with the package."

"Thank you again, for last night. He's really excited that someone is taking his art seriously. I appreciate your help with him. I feel like I don't even know how to talk to him anymore. I'm not his parent, but I'm..."

"The only one doing the job?"

She nods and keeps her eyes on the ground. "Our dad...he's got PTSD. He has a hard time holding down a job. He's okay for a little while, and then he starts..."

"I saw the beer cans, Cherry. I get it. Is he a veteran?"

"Yeah. They send a little money every month, but he should be getting more, I think. His hand is really messed up. I think the pain from that and the PTSD...it didn't help that my mom left us." She shakes her head. "Sorry. You probably don't need to hear all of this."

I put my arm around her shoulders. "I do need to hear all of this. I get the feeling you've been carrying all the weight of your family since your mom lit out?"

She nods.

"My dad left after Dillon was born. I know how it is to grow up with one parent. You've been handling it much better than I did. I caused my mom even more trouble. I was wild. When I wasn't sullen."

She peeks up at me. "That's pretty much how Adam has been since she left. I don't know how to help him. Or save him from himself. And dad isn't much help."

I've never had a savior complex before, but Cherry is bringing it out in me. I want to help her as much as I want want to fuck her. My mind is spinning with options about spending time with Adam, giving him the kind of male influence that would have been helpful to me when I was his age. And maybe even looking into how to get Cherry's dad the help he needs. I know there are organizations that help veterans get the benefits they deserve. And if money has been keeping him from rehab, I could help there too. Though it's not always that simple.

What the hell is going on with me? She might not even want my help.

We stop at the door to the bookstore. Cherry smiles and pulls out the key I gave her last night. Her smile is brighter than the sun. I'm so drawn to her, I can barely think of anything else.

A man is walking down the street toward us. He looks like a frat boy who has forgotten that he's not in college anymore. He's wearing a polo shirt with a popped collar and khaki shorts. He has an air of superiority about him, as if he believes that the world is his own private playground.

And he's frowning at us.

He stops, and Cherry's body visibly tenses, eyes narrowed and jaw clenched. Her hands ball into fists at her side and her face is set with a determination that wasn't there before.

"Cherry, what's going on here?" he says. "Is this man bothering you?" he asks.

What the actual fuck?

"Hi, Chad."

He waits for an explanation. Like it's his due.

She exhales, realizing he isn't going away. *If she wants him to go away, I can damn well make that happen.*

"Chad, this is Max Duke. Max owns this store." The preppy asshole looks like he just stepped in dog shit. "Max," she nods her head at the man almost reluctantly, "this is Chad Hamilton. Mayor Hamilton's son."

Well, hell.

Seven

Cherry

This is so awkward.

The men size each other up in the doorway of the bookstore. Chad Hamilton, mayor's son, entitled ass whose daddy runs the town and hates Max. Max Duke, the town bad boy trying to rehab downtown even though he's going to get trouble from the old town cronies led by Chad's father.

"Nice to meet you, Chad," Max lies.

Chad sneers. "I've heard all about you, Duke. Cherry, I'll ask you again. Is this man bothering you?"

Like Chad is some kind of hero protecting my honor. The guy who bullied me for most of my childhood.

Max scowls and steps forward, towering over Chad. His broad shoulders make him look like a mountain compared to Chad's almost wiry frame.

Chad takes a step back, intimidated by Max's sheer power and strength. His eyes dart around nervously as if just now realizing he's outmatched. Duh, Chad.

Max steps closer, his biceps bulging as he crosses his arms over his broad chest, his dominance radiating off him in waves. His presence fills the street with his undeniable authority, making it clear who the alpha is in this situation. Probably any situation.

Most definitely the bedroom situation, I bet. Which sends tingles to some places that shouldn't be tingling right now.

My gaze travels down Max's body, taking in the tight jeans that hug his muscular thighs, the black t-shirt that shows off his toned chest and arms, the big shitkicker boots that cover his feet. I want to rip those clothes off him and have my way with him right here on the street.

Max looks at me, his eyes darkening as he takes in my expression. He knows what I'm thinking, what I want to do to him, and it only makes me want to do it more. His lips curl into a smirk as if he's daring me to make a move.

I'm not really a dare kind of girl. But Max brings out something inside me. Some kind of vixen. And part of me wants to show Chad once and for all to leave me alone.

I step forward, closing the distance between Max and me. Our bodies almost touching, the heat between us undisguised.

Both men are waiting for me to answer Chad's question.

"No, Chad. He's not bothering me," I say, though I don't look at Chad. I can't take my eyes off Max. "Not the way you're asking anyway."

Max's hands find their way to my waist, pulling me closer to him. "We're a little busy, Chad. But it was nice to meet you."

He doesn't wait for a response from Chad, instead he pulls me into the bookstore and closes the door behind us, pushing me against it.

I'm trapped in Max's arms. How many times have I fantasized about wall kisses? The kind in my romance novels. His body is hot against mine, and all I can think about is how badly I want him.

Max's lips find mine, and all thoughts of Chad and romance novels and the outside world disappear. His kiss is hard and demanding, and I melt into him. I wrap my arms around his neck, pulling him closer, and he moans into my mouth.

He breaks the kiss, and I whimper at the loss of contact. "I've been wanting to do this all morning," Max says, his voice low and husky.

I'm barely able to respond as his lips trail down my neck, leaving a trail of fire in their wake. His hands roam over my body, gripping my hips and pulling me even closer to him. I can feel the hard length of him against me, and I moan at the sensation.

"Max," I gasp, my fingers tangling in his hair.

He lifts me up, and I wrap my legs around his waist as he carries me to the back of the store where we won't be seen through the windows. He sets me down on a table and continues to kiss me hungrily, his hands exploring my body as I arch against him.

I'm lost in the feel of him, in his touch and his kiss. His hands move up my thighs and push my dress up toward my waist.

Thoughts try to make their way through my brain. I remember that I need to tell him. "Max, wait."

He pauses. "Are you okay?" he asks, concern evident in his voice.

I nod. "I need to tell you something."

"Okay."

Before I can say anything else, Max looks at me with such raw desire that I forget what I was going to say.

"I can't remember now–"

Max's lips crash against mine, cutting off my words. His hands grip my hips as he grinds into me, letting me feel how aroused he is. His kisses become more urgent and desperate, and the wetness between my legs grows.

I moan into his mouth. "Wait, I remember now."

"What is it baby," he asks, moving his drugging kisses to my neck.

"I love it when you kiss my neck like that," I whisper.

"Then I'll never stop," he murmurs, pushing my dress down my shoulders and kissing a path down my chest to the tops of my breasts.

I'm lost in the pleasure of his touch, in the feel of his body against mine. I never want this to end.

"That wasn't what I needed to tell you. That was an aside. Sorry."

He chuckles against my skin, and though I can tell it costs him, he takes a step back. His eyes darken as he looks at me. I think about what I must look like to him, my dress bunched up to my waist while falling off my shoulders. My hair mussed from his hands. My lips swollen from his kisses.

"If you keep looking at me like that, I'm going to forget again," I say.

"Maybe that's what I want," he says, grinning.

"I just wanted to tell you...before we go too far...there's something you need to know about me."

"Okay..."

I close my eyes. Maybe I shouldn't tell him. Maybe if I don't say anything, he won't even notice. No. I need to be honest. He might not want the responsibility–

"Cherry," he interrupts my rambling thoughts.

"Sorry. It's just that..."

"Do you not want to go any further? I'm not trying to rush you." He scrapes a hand through his hair, and a rush of moisture soaks my panties again. I don't know why that movement was so hot. Something about a man as cool as Max being on the edge of losing his cool because of me. Because Chubby Cherry makes him so crazy with desire.

But he's waiting for my announcement. The one that might push him away.

I take a deep breath. "You're not rushing me. It's just that...well..."

"Spit it out, woman."

"It's just that I haven't done this before."

"Done what before?" he asks, clearly perplexed.

"Gone past first base, really."

He steps back, shocked. "Are you telling me–"

"I'm telling you, Max, that I'm still a virgin."

Eight

Max

I don't think I heard her correctly.

I look at the goddess sitting on the table in front of me looking half-dressed and freshly fucked already and can't make sense of the words she just said.

"What do you mean, you're a virgin?"

Cherry's cheeks flush pink as she bites her lip nervously. "The usual definition. I've never been with a man before," she admits, her voice barely above a whisper.

I'm stunned. Cherry is the most beautiful woman I've ever laid eyes on, and the thought of her being untouched is hard to believe. My cock throbs at the thought of being her first.

Her only.

She looks up at me with wide eyes, and I can see the fear mixed with desire in them. I take her face in my hands and press my lips to hers, kissing her deeply. She melts into me, perfect trust already.

I pull back and gaze into her eyes, my heart pounding in my chest. "Why have you waited?" I whisper gruffly, my voice barely audible.

Me. You were waiting for me.

She smiles shyly and looks away. "No one in Tempest was...I just wanted something I haven't found."

"What do you want, sweetheart?"

"I don't think I know. I want...I don't really know."

My mind flashes to our conversation last night about her fantasy. Cherry doesn't want to be wooed gently or rescued. Cherry wants to be plundered.

She needs a man that can take control of the situation, maybe because she's had so much responsibility thrust on her at such an early age, maybe because she's shy and needs help breaking out of her shell. She needs a man who can make her fantasies come true.

And I am that man.

I stand up with a newfound desire to take control and show her just how beautiful surrendering to me can be. My gaze is intense and she swallows hard, understanding the unspoken words between us.

An instinct as natural as breathing and as old as time itself takes over me. My body surges with adrenaline, every nerve tingling with anticipation. I know what she needs. I know what *I* need.

She shyly pulls up the bodice of her dress to cover her shoulders again, but I yank it back down, trapping her arms in the fabric. She blinks, surprised.

"Your body belongs to me now," I tell her, my voice low and commanding. "I like looking at it." She inhales sharply, her eyes widening. I cup her breast through the fabric of her dress, tweaking her nipple between my thumb and finger. She arches her back, pressing her chest into my hand. "I'm finally beginning to understand you, Cherry. You crave a man who is strong enough to take control, isn't that right?"

She looks at me timidly and nods.

I continue, "You long for a man who knows your body's needs and desires without you having to tell him what they are."

She looks away shyly and nods again.

"I want to be that man for you, Cherry. I want to be the man who can do all the things to you that you've been dreaming of. I want to make you mine."

Her breathing is shallow, and she swallows hard. "But you could have anyone you want," she whispers. "Why do you want me?"

I want to lighten the mood a little since she seems to be feeling a lack of confidence. I lean in and brush my lips against her ear. "Because you're the only beautiful woman I've ever met with such a dirty, dirty mind."

She chuckles in surprise at that. "I don't have a dirty mind." I love that chuckle. I want to make her laugh almost as much as I want to make her come.

"Oh, I think you do have a dirty mind. I think you are a very wicked girl who wants to do very bad things. Dirty things."

She blushes and looks away, hiding her face. I grip her chin with my thumb and forefinger, tugging her head back to face me. Forcing her to acknowledge what she wants.

"What dirty things do you think I want?" she asks, almost sassy about it.

"You want to be fucked hard. You want to be taken. You want to be bent over my knee and spanked until you're wet and begging for my cock."

I can see the desire in her eyes, even as she shakes her head. "I don't do those things."

"But you think about them. And I'm going to make sure you get everything you want. Everything you need."

Her pulse throbs in her neck, and I lean in to lick it. She exhales a choked sob and grabs my shirt in her fists, clinging to me desperately. I move my lips over her jawline and kiss the corner of her mouth. She moans as I nibble on her lower lip, and then I take it in my mouth and suck on it.

She shivers, understanding in her eyes. She knows that what she has been waiting for is finally here. Like someone has finally turned the key to all of the fantasies she has kept hidden deep inside her.

"That's why you waited, didn't give your body to anyone else," I growl, my voice thick and gruff to match the desire coursing through me. "You knew I'd find you. You waited for me. Only me."

She's not the only one whose desires have been unlocked. Needs I didn't know I had course through me. Primal needs.

To protect. To fuck. To claim.

Nothing and no one will stand between us. This woman is my destiny.

She gulps nervously. "You're not mad, even a little? I just thought maybe you'd want someone more experienced," she says quietly. "I don't know how to do stuff. How to please you. I know you're used to a different kind of woman."

"There's only one kind of woman for me now," I tell her in a low, husky voice. "Everything about you pleases me."

"But I don't know how to..." she protests.

"You don't need to know how," I reply instantly, brushing my thumb across her cheek. "I'll guide you through everything. It will be my pleasure. And yours. Do you trust me?"

She nods, looking relieved. "I trust you."

"Good girl."

My heart thuds heavily in my chest and I know we're on the verge of something new. Something neither of us have experienced before.

I slide my lips against hers, my two desires battling against one another. To protect her and to ravish her. But I know what she needs and what she wants. She needs me to be fierce and take control while keeping her safe from the outside world.

I'll never protect Cherry from my desire for her though.

When it comes to my need for her, she'll only ever get the full force of my passion. I won't hold back–that's what she wants. That's what she needs.

My cock throbs against my pants. "I'm going to give you everything you need, Cherry. "

I'm not just talking about sex. I'm talking about every part of her life. I'm going to be her savior. Her protector. I'll take care of her and make sure she's always happy.

And her rough lover, when she needs it.

I kiss her long and hard, like I want to rip off all of her clothes right now. To peel off every layer, until she's totally bare and vulnerable. I want to claim her. To show her who she belongs to.

But I force myself to slow down. This isn't the place or the time. But I can sure as fuck tease her.

"One day soon, I'm going to fuck you until you can't think straight, and you won't be able to get enough of me." She gasps at my declaration, but I'm not done. "I'm going to make you feel things you never knew were possible, and when I'm done with you, you'll be begging for more."

"Um. Someday? Not...now?" Her face is such a delicious shade of pink.

"I wish, but no. Not here. Not today." I move my hand down her body, gripping her ass and pulling her towards me. She moans, opening her mouth to mine. I plunge my tongue inside her, tasting her.

Her fingers dig into my back, and she pulls me closer to her. I press myself against her, my cock aching.

"I want to fuck you Cherry," I growl, pulling away from her lips to whisper in her ear. "I want to fill you up with my come."

"Okay," she says, looking a little sheepish.

But I'm not done. It's time to push her out of her boundaries.

"I want you to tell me how much you want me to make you come."

"I...don't think I can."

I wrap her hair around my hand and pull a little. Just a little. "Say it," I demand.

She swallows hard. "I want you to make me come so hard," she whispers.

I smile. "That's right, dirty girl. Tell me how much you want my cock inside you."

"I want your cock," she gasps, her voice husky. "I want your cock so badly."

"Where do you want it, sweetheart?" She stares at me, her eyes wide, and I know I have to give her more direction. "Say it."

She bites her lip and looks away. "I want you to put your cock in my pussy," she whispers, her cheeks bright red.

"That's right," I growl, my cock so fucking hard I can barely stand it. "You want my cock in your tight little pussy."

I'm throbbing with need, and I can't wait to show her just what we're going to do. But not here. Not now.

She shifts, and I study her.

"You want it so bad you're squirming in your seat, aren't you?"

She nods, her eyes wide.

"Would you like me to do something about it?"

She nods again, but doesn't know what to ask for.

"I'm going to get you off, sweetheart." I rub the outside of her drenched panties.

"Oh, God," she moans, throwing back her head and closing her eyes.

My heart pounds as I slide my fingers under her panties, through her wet heat. "Do you want me to make you come?"

She nods frantically, her eyes still closed. I can't believe how wet she is. "Sweetheart," I murmur, sliding a finger in and out of her wet slit. "Open your eyes and look at me."

She opens her eyes. They're dark as storm clouds now.

"That's right," I murmur, sliding one finger inside and rubbing her clit with my thumb. "God, you're so fucking wet, baby. So ready for me."

I circle my thumb over her clit and slide a second finger inside her. She gasps and moans, her back arching as I tease her, bringing her closer and closer to the edge.

"That's it," I murmur, increasing the pressure and speed of my fingers. "Come for me, sweetheart."

She whimpers as she explodes in my arms, her walls clamping down around my fingers pleasure rolls through her body. I keep up the pressure until the last shiver has died away and then gently pull out my fingers. She collapses against me with a sigh.

"You did so good," I murmur against her ear.

"Thank you," she replies, her breathing gradually slowing.

She looks drunk with pleasure, but I'm not done yet.

She straightens, blinking away the fog of pleasure. I lick my fingers clean and her eyes widen.

"I wanted to taste you."

Her face flushes bright red.

"So fucking sweet. You'll see." I smile at her shock. "Someday, I'm going to make you come, and then I'm going to watch you lick your own juices off my cock."

She moans and I grin, putting her dress back to rights. "So let's finish this inspection of the bookstore and get to lunch. I'm starving."

"What?" Dazed confusion laces her voice.

"You wanted to walk through the space so you can pick a name for the store, remember? And then we're going to grab a bite to eat and figure out your book budget."

"My book budget," she repeats in a dazed voice.

"After that, I need to figure out which of the houses I'm going to move into so we can have some privacy, and I can keep you in my bed for hours and hours."

"Max..."

"When I get you in that bed, I'm going to touch you, taste you, make you come over and over again. And I'm going to take my time so you can get ready for my cock." I grasp her chin and kiss the top of her head. "So let's get going."

She doesn't speak again, but I know my words are going to be playing over and over in her head all afternoon. Tormenting her. Tormenting me.

Nine

Cherry

I'm not used to being a regular diner at the diner. It's weird to be sitting at a table and being waited on instead of on my feet and bringing food out.

Weirder still that I'm sitting with Max Duke. The hottest man I've ever met. The man who just fingered me to orgasm half an hour ago. The man who knows my darkest desires and my lifelong dreams. And insists he wants to give me both.

And the man who is my boss.

We're looking on his tablet at some different inventory and point-of-sale software options. And waiting for our lunch. I'm so excited about opening the bookstore, but I'm also very distracted by the thoughts of what we were just doing in it.

As we discuss the software options, I can't help but sneak glances at Max. I think of the intimate way he touched me earlier. The way he played me like an instrument. I had no idea it could be like that, even in my dark fantasies. I'm lost in thought when I feel his hand on my thigh. I startle, look at his hand and then look up at him, and he's smirking at me.

"You're a little distracted, Cherry. By any chance, are you thinking about what we did earlier?" he asks.

I bite my lip. "Maybe a little," I reply, my voice barely above a whisper.

He leans in closer to me. "Are you thinking about my fingers inside you?"

I can feel the heat radiating from my face as I look up at him. "Yes," I admit.

"Me too," Max tells me, taking a long drink of his iced tea.

I shoot him a look, meaning to tell him he's incorrigible. Instead, we lock eyes and I feel my pussy grow wet again. It's like this primal need to have sex with him has flooded my system, and it's making me crazy with lust.

"Stop looking at me," I beg. "You're making me more distracted."

He just smiles like the cat that ate the canary. "I have no idea what you mean."

Mary, my diner boss, stops at the table with our food. She's giving me an unreadable look. "Mary, you know Max," I say, though the most notorious bad boy Tempest has ever seen needs no introduction.

"I remember Max," she replies dubiously.

"Mary," Max smiles. "I've traveled the country and no one makes a lemon meringue better than yours."

"Quit kissing my butt, Duke. I hear you're taking my best waitress away from me."

I duck my chin to my chest. I hate that I'm leaving her. She's been so good to me. But she would be the first to tell me to follow my dreams. And running a bookstore has always been my dream.

"I'll make sure I bring her by several times a week for lunch," he promises.

"I'm not going anywhere. I'm just down the street," I laugh. "Seriously, Mary. Now I can order all the cozy mystery books your heart desires."

Luckily, Rachel, one of our other waitresses, has been wanting more hours. She's thrilled to have my shifts, so I didn't even have to give two weeks notice. With the contract I signed this morning, I start getting paid today.

Mary is still giving Max the side-eye. "What are your intentions toward Cherry?"

"Mary!" I protest.

"She's not like those tarts who throw themselves at you."

I cover my face. with my hands. "Mary, please."

Max chuckles. "I know Cherry is special. I've only known her for a day, and I know. If anyone is in danger here, it's me."

Mary makes a snorting sound and walks away. I expect I'll have to fill her in more later when we're alone. A lot has happened since I clocked out of my shift yesterday.

I peek at Max through my fingers. He seems sincere. I don't understand what would be the point of coming to town and pretending to like me. Pretending to make every single one of my dreams come true. He's even helped me ease my problems with my little brother.

At some point, I might just have to accept the fact that as weird as it may seem, Max is on the level and he really likes me.

As soon as Mary is out of earshot, Max apologizes if he embarrassed me. "She's like a mama bear, that one," he says. "But I meant what I said. I've meant everything I've said to you."

I pick up my sandwich but put it down again. "Max, why? I know you came back to Tempest to rebuild it. But why are you being so nice to me? You're practically giving me a bookstore."

"You can have it if you want. I'll sign over the ownership."

"Max, stop. You've known me for one day. You can't just give me a building and a business. I'm serious. You helped me with my brother last night, you gave me my dream job, and you ...well, you know."

"Made you come on my hand?" he fills in for me.

The blush is hot and instant. "Yes, that."

"I told you I meant everything I've said to you. Including everything I said when you were writhing on my fingers."

"Max." Memories of him murmuring his desires for me echo in my mind. The dominant way he spoke made my heart race and my body hum with pleasure.

He smiles evilly. "I love making you blush, sweetheart."

"The things you said earlier. In the heat of the moment. I'm not going to hold you to them–"

"Stop right there. I meant all that too. I knew the instant I saw you that we belonged together." He waits for me to look him in the eye. "But it wasn't just that moment that told me. That was physical. But we're more than that. I knew we belonged together when you stood by my side yesterday, risking your reputation. I knew when we had our date last night. I knew when you let me help you with your brother. I knew when you told me you were a virgin but let me make you come."

I want to believe him. I want to believe everything he's saying. But I can't. "I'm a common waitress. You're the famous Max Duke. I can't imagine you want someone like me."

He puts his hand over my mouth to shut me up. "Nothing about you is common to me. I want to know everything about you."

"Everything?" I breathe out against his hand.

"I want to know what makes you happy. I want to know what makes you sad. What makes you wet. Your favorite color, flower, movie, book, food. Everything."

"Max," I whisper, breathless and overwhelmed.

He takes his hand away. "Say you believe me. Say you're mine, and I'll give you everything you have ever wanted or needed."

I gulp. "I already told you today that I was yours. "

"Yes, you did. Why don't you tell me again? Right now. Not when I'm distracting you with orgasms."

I kick him lightly under the table. "I've always believed in love at first sight, Maxwell Duke. I just didn't believe it would ever happen to me. Not really." I push my plate away. "When my mama left us, I just assumed it's because I wasn't worth much." My hands start shaking, so I wring them under the table where he can't see. "And it didn't get better with time. I got teased a lot growing up. About my weight. About being poor. Hell, about being smart. I have a lot of scars, and I don't think I'm going to be very easy to love."

"Babe, if you think I'm very easy to love..."

"You are! Look how you came back to town and invested in its future even though they treated you bad before you left and you owe Tempest nothing. You stood up to the mayor, something nobody ever does. You treated my brother with respect even though he was arrested for vandalism and interrupted our first date. You...well...you made me feel desirable, something I've never felt my whole life."

I don't think I'm going to win the battle against the tears threatening to make an appearance. I don't want to cry. Not in the diner. Not where everyone will assume Max is making me cry. But I'm getting choked up.

"I've never wanted anyone like I want you, Cherry. I swear."

"I have to believe you because after I said all those nice things about you, I realize you're not a liar." I take a deep breath. "But you should know, if you plan on breaking my heart, I know a woman who lives just outside of town who sells hexes really cheap."

He laughs. "How much do hexes run these days?"

"Her normal price is $25, but if you want to hex a man, she takes ten percent off because she hates men."

"All right." He waves Mary over and opens his wallet. "Mary," he hands her a twenty and a five dollar bill, "will you put this in an envelope and keep it someplace safe if Cherry ever needs it? It's hex insurance."

Mary shakes her head. "I don't know what your deal is, Max Duke, but I'm taking this money to bingo tonight."

She takes his money and walks away. I can't stop giggling.

Max looks at his phone. "I have some more errands. You have the key, so after you finish here, go figure out if you need any repairs or renovations at the bookstore. And pick a name." He kisses the top of my head. "I'll pay the check on my way out. I'll call you later."

"Bye."

I feel everyone in the diner staring at me. They all know me as their sweet, quiet waitress. Someone who's more like a fixture in the restaurant than a person. And they know Max Duke as a rebellious troublemaker who left town in a cloud of mystery and returned years later much the same. What they don't know what to do with is the sight of us together as a couple.

I don't know what to do with it either

I sit there, stirring the straw in my tea for a few more minutes. This could really be my life now. I'm torn between letting it happen and putting up walls to make sure I don't get hurt.

I finally get myself down the street to the bookstore and see a motorcycle in front. I open the door.

"Max?" I call out.

Instead of Max, a man I don't know comes out of the back room holding a saw.

A very big man. A very big saw.

The big man holding a saw smiles at me. "Don't freak out, okay? I'm William Duke."

I let out my breath in a whoosh. "Max's brother." Not a serial killer. Which is nice since things finally seem to be going my way for a change. It would suck to be hacked into a million pieces today.

Dillon nods. "Max told me to come by and fix some trim." "Oh."

As I look at William, I can't help but notice the similarities between him and Max. They share the same broad shoulders and strong jawline. They move the same, even. William is handsome, but Max exudes a raw, primal energy that leaves me weak in the knees.

I follow him back into the back room where he's been working.

"You're Cherry?" he asks, though he knows. He's trying to aim for polite conversation, which is hard for me because I keep looking at the table where not that long ago, I had my first orgasm with another human being present.

"Sorry. Yes. I'm Cherry Miller, the new bookstore manager Max hired."

Dillon laughs. "You're more than that. My brother is already whipped. That's a new sight to see. I'm glad to meet the woman who finally got to him."

Got to him?

"Max told you about me?"

He nods. "I think you're the only woman he's ever mentioned more than once. And he talks nonstop. Cherry this, Cherry that." He smiles, and I feel my cheeks flush with warmth. "He said you are sweet, smart, and the woman he's going to marry."

My heart thuds. I can't believe Max would talk about me like that.

"Well, um, thank you," I stammer out. I try to hide my blush and smile awkwardly at Dillon instead. "We just met yesterday. He's moving pretty fast."

He grins back. "Of course he is. He's Max. That's what he does. That's part of the reason we were always in so much trouble growing up."

"Just part of the reason?"

"I'm more methodical. Given the chance, I prefer to think things through a little more. But our youngest brother, Dillon, worshiped Max and would have followed him over a cliff. So I had to go along to protect him. I'm not saying we didn't have fun. Just that Max was the instigator." He pauses. "Max is right, you are easy to talk to. I don't usually say much."

The compliment means a lot to me. I'm not used to praise.

"Hey, Cherry, do you want to know some embarrassing stories about Max?"

"Do I ever," I reply.

Dillon and I spend an hour going over funny stories about the brothers and their troublemaking youth while he stains some trim.

When he leaves, I check my phone for the time. Adam gets out of school soon and I want to be home when he gets there. I have time to work on my business plan for half an hour and that makes me happier than it sounds.

Max told me I need to map out the details of my bookstore, including the type of books I plan to sell, my target market, my pricing strategy, and my marketing plan. We looked at possible point-of-sale programs today, but before we can set up accounts with distributors so I can order books (oh my God, I get to order books) we need a business license. But we can't get one until I pick a name.

I've gone through all the cutesy names, the puns, and using "Cherry" in the title, but I think I want something more solid.

I text Max. "Is Tempest Books too boring? I want to use the town name in the title. Since we're working to brand the whole town, not just the store."

He answers. "Love it."

When I get home, the first thing I notice is that it smells like food. Even when my dad is sober, he doesn't cook. Adam is actually a good cook, but he's not supposed to be home yet.

"Adam?" I call out as I walk through the house into the kitchen. "So help me, if you skipped school today—"

My words are cut off by the sight of my boss, ex boss, Mary.

"What's going on?" I ask. "Where's my dad? What are you doing here?"

Ten

Cherry

"Relax, child," Mary tells me. "Sit."

I take a seat.

"Your dad is fine. He's in the shower trying to sober up a little." I'm taken aback. "He called me," she continues. "We've been friends for a long time. But...closer this last year or so."

How could I have no idea that my boss and my dad even knew each other? It's no secret my dad is a drunk, but I didn't realize he talked to anyone about it other than his sponsor.

Wait a minute...

Mary sees when it dawns on me that she's his sponsor. "I didn't know you..."

"I haven't had a drink since before you were born. But I still go to meetings. I still sponsor."

"Thank you for being there for him. I don't know what to do anymore." Mary places her hand on mine, and I feel a wave of relief wash over me. "Can I ask you something?" I say, looking up at her.

"Of course, anything."

"Do you think it's possible for someone to change? I mean, really change?" I ask, thinking about my dad and his constant struggle with alcoholism.

Mary leans back in her chair, thinking for a moment. "Yes, I do. It's not easy, but it's possible. Your dad has to want to change, though. And he has to put in the effort to make it

71

happen. But with the right support and resources, it's definitely possible."

"You did it."

"I did it."

I've never talked to anyone about my struggles before. About my dad. "I can't help but think about the past, and how my dad used to be before the alcohol took over. He used to be a good man, a loving father. But now, he's a shell of his former self. Since my mom left us. Maybe before. When he came back from the war. I don't know. I get my memories mixed up sometimes."

"You were just a kid, Cherry."

I sniff the air. "That smells amazing."

"I brought over some soup from the diner. Your dad wants to go to rehab. Well, want is a stretch. But we found a bed. They can take him tonight. "

"This is his third time," I voice, wondering how I'm going to juggle it all by myself. Again. "Maybe I shouldn't have quit my job at the diner. I don't have time to learn a whole new career and—"

"It's going to be okay. I didn't know about all the weight you were carrying. You must have still been in school when he went to rehab the first two times. I didn't realize until today that nobody has been helping you. I'm so sorry we all let you down."

"It's not your job to take care of me either. But yes, I was still in school when he went, the first time anyway."

"And you took care of Adam by yourself?"

"I didn't want anyone to take him away."

My shoulders start to shake and Mary gets up and comes around to hug me.

"Oh, child. Alright. This is how it is going to go. Adam will stay with me on the weekends. And I'll send over meals during the week so you can concentrate on work."

"That's too much, Mary."

"It's not."

Adam comes into the kitchen, sniffing the air like I did. "What smells so good?"

"Mary made us soup."

And then I tell him about Dad.

• • • •

THE NEXT DAY I GET a text from Max to meet him at his new house.

That guy works fast.

We'd spent a few hours earlier in the day filling out online forms for the business license. We hit Pinterest, a first for Max, to come up with branding ideas and signage. He went off to work on his other bazillion projects to rehab downtown, and I fine-tuned the business plan and got Adam over to Mary's since it was Friday.

Dad left last night. Adam was gone for the weekend. I was free. I've never only had to worry about myself.

I take a long bath. Do a honey face mask from a recipe I found while we were pinning. Shave my legs. And worry.

Is tonight the night? Am I ready?

I arrive at the address Max sent me. A cute little bungalow on Cherry St. of all things.

Max opens the front door as I'm walking toward it. My breath catches. He's so sexy and I can't even stand it.

It's like he stepped out of my wildest dreams. He has on a pair of jeans with a tight yet another black t-shirt that clings to his body and tree trunk biceps. His hair is slicked back, fresh from the shower, giving me a brand new fantasy to think about–Max in the shower, soap cascading down his chest to the deep V of his...

He smiles at me and steps aside, allowing me to enter the house. "Thanks for coming," he says softly, his deep voice sending shivers down my spine.

He closes the door and pushes me against it, his body pressing tightly against mine. My heart races as he leans down to capture my lips in a hungry kiss. I moan against his mouth as his hands roam over my body, sending sparks of pleasure through my veins.

Max breaks the kiss, his breath hot against my neck as he presses his body harder against mine. "God, Cherry, I can't stop thinking about you," he whispers, his lips trailing kisses down my neck. I tilt my head back, giving him better access as I let out a soft whimper.

He pulls away, his eyes searching mine. "I know we agreed to take things slow but it's killing me."

I blink at him and blink in confusion. "I don't think I agreed to take things slow. That was all you. "

"Too bad," he says. "Come see my house."

There's...not much in it. Until we get to the master bedroom. Which consists of one large bed already made up with a fluffy duvet and ..."That's a lot of pillows, Max."

"Women like pillows. You're always putting them everywhere. I wanted you to never want to get out of my bed once I get you in it."

"Well, I'm free for the next forty-eight hours."

His grin is absolutely evil. "Well, first, I'm going to feed you. And then, I'm going to feast on you."

Eleven

Max

The sweet blush on Cherry's face is gratifying as fuck. She's had me in absolute knots since I met her. I like knowing she's just as affected by the whole situation as I am, that she wants me just as much as I want her.

I have takeout in the kitchen, so I take her hand and lead her there. "Sorry I don't have any chairs yet. Or any other furniture."

Her tinkling laugh lightens my heart. "Max, you didn't even have a house when I last saw you a few hours ago. I'd say you're moving along at an impressive clip."

I grab the food and let her out the kitchen door where there is a bench. "I've owned this house for a month or so. Or I should say, our company owns this house. But yeah, I had to pick which one I was moving into today and then go find a furniture store to get a bed."

She swallows a bite. "What made you choose this house?"

"Proximity to downtown. I don't think it's my forever house, though."

"No? Are you going to build something?"

I shake my head. "I think I'd like to renovate my old house. The one my brothers and I grew up in. It's been left vacant too long and needs a lot of updating, but it's a solid old house. They don't make them like that anymore. I have a few things to work out though, before I decide."

"What things?" she asks, taking a drink.

"Well, I need your input."

Her eyes widen and her mouth hangs open. "Mine?"

"Cherry, you haven't been paying attention if that surprises you."

"Max–"

I interrupt her before she can finish whatever it is she was going to say. "When we get married–"

"Married!" She screeches the word

I start again. "When we get married, I want to give you all your dreams. I can't just pick a house without your input."

"Max–"

I lean in and cut her off with a kiss. I know Cherry feels the same way I do. She's just not used to my full-speed-ahead attitude to life yet. She's a lot more cautious. She's had to be. Which is part of the reason I like riling her up.

When we break apart, Cherry is panting and her eyes are glazed over with desire. "Max, I–"

I put my finger over her lips. "It's not a proposal. You deserve a real proposal. One to rival your childhood dreams about me. But you should know that's the direction we are headed. Wedding, house, babies, porch swings. The whole thing."

She stares at me, her eyes wide and unblinking. I can tell she's processing what I just said. "We've only known each other for two days."

I continue my speech, trying to keep my voice calm and steady. "We can renovate the old house and turn it into something beautiful. Something that we both love. But I want us to work together on this. I want you to be happy, Cherry. I want to make all your dreams come true."

I distract her by changing the subject to the bookstore while we finish dinner. *That* subject doesn't freak her out. She's so cute when she's talking about what she wants to do with the space.

"I'm rambling," she apologizes.

"I like it. But I am getting hungry."

She screws up her face, obviously confused. "You just finished eating your dinner."

"I'm ready for my dessert, Cherry." I lick my lips suggestively. "I'm ready to feast on you."

There's that blush again. "I thought you said you wanted to take it slow? I mean physically. I thought you didn't want to have sex with me yet."

"Oh, I do want to have sex with you. Very much. I'm just not going to fuck you tonight." She gets this cute little wrinkle in her forehead. "But I'm going to make you come over and over again."

Cherry inhales sharply and bites her lip. "When you talk that way...I think I like it more than I should. More than I'm supposed to."

I kiss her hand. "When I talk dirty, you mean?"

She nods.

"Sweetheart, what happens when we're alone is just between you and me. There's no should or shouldn't as long as you're happy." I lead her back into the house, into the bedroom. "I know you're a good girl and I know you're a bad girl. I want all of you. Both parts and everything in between."

I start by lightly kissing the back of her neck, my hands freeing her messy bun. Her soft tresses cascade down her shoulders like a curtain of silk. She quivers as I move my mouth to her ear and nibble on the lobe.

"Max," she whispers, her voice shaking with desire.

"Tell me if you want me to stop. "

"I don't think I ever want you to stop."

"Good girl. "

My hands move to the buttons of her dress, undoing them one at a time until I can slide the fabric down over her curves and let it pool around her feet. She stands before me wearing nothing but a pair of panties and bra and she looks absolutely breathtaking.

I unhook her bra while looking deeply into her eyes. She brings up a hand to hold it in place, looking a little wary.

I don't like that look. That means she's scared, and it's my job to keep her from ever needing to be scared again.

"What's going on, sweetheart?"

"I've been teased about my breasts," she whispers. "They developed early, and I've always felt insecure about them. The kids at school...even some grown-ups...they're too big. They're ugly and they make me look cheap."

Her words break my heart, and I feel rage building inside me at the thought of anyone ever making her feel bad about her body. I cup her breasts gently and kiss the tops of them reverently.

"Cherry, you are so beautiful," I whisper against her skin. "Your body is perfect."

She looks up at me with tears in her eyes, and I cup her face with my hands and kiss away the tears.

I continue to kiss and caress her, letting her know that she is beautiful and desirable and that I will never make her feel anything but loved.

"You don't have to be embarrassed or ashamed of your body, sweetheart. You are flawless in every way. And tonight, I'm going to show you just how much I love your body."

She drops her hand and the bra falls to the floor. Her eyes close tight, as if she's mentally bracing herself for my response.

"You are perfect," I tell her, my voice low and husky with desire. "Just perfect."

My hands gently explore her curves, tracing each like I'm drawing a picture. And then, when my mouth finally touches her breasts, I worship them with every lick, suck and nibble. I press my lips against her skin and breathe in the scent of her as she quivers under my mouth.

Mine.

My hands caress her back and hips as I devour her nipples until she can't take it anymore, shivering in pleasure as moans escape her lips.

I take my time kissing and licking my way down her body. I slide her panties off at last, taking a moment to appreciate the beauty of her pussy before trailing a finger down the center of it. She gasps out at the sensation.

"I love how responsive you are."

I kneel down in front of her and kiss the inside of each thigh, tracing a line with my tongue up to the apex between them. I'm eager as fuck to taste her, but I want to tease us both a little more.

"Not yet," I whisper against her as I move my mouth up to her generous tummy, gently nibbling as I go, her gasps encouraging my exploration. I make my way back up to her chest, kissing and licking my way up until I reach her breasts. I suck and tease her nipples again, playing with them as I learn what she likes.

"Baby, I'm going to make you come so hard," I whisper, the words filled with promise.

She sighs, her body trembling with desire. "I can't wait," she breathes. "You're wearing too many clothes, Max."

"I'm afraid I won't be able to control myself if I take them off." If my cock comes out, there's no way I can stop. As it is, I'll probably come in my jeans when I go down on her.

She tugs on my clothes. "At least take off your shirt?"

"You like my body, naughty girl?"

"So much, Max. Please?"

I stand and pull off my shirt. She gratifies me with the cutest feminine growl, and then her hands are on me. She can't seem to get enough of my bare skin. She traces my abs and chest, getting acquainted with my body.

I love every second of it. "Sweetheart, tonight is about you. Your pleasure."

"Then let me keep touching you," she says huskily.

The tone of her voice makes my cock strain against my jeans. That fucker wants out.

Cherry adds her mouth to her exploration of my torso, and I growl. She traces around my nipple with her tongue and my knees want to buckle.

"Fuck, " I moan and grab hold of her hair to keep her there. The sensation of her mouth on my nipples is enough to make me come. Like there's a direct line right to my cock. "Fuck," I say again, wrapping my hand in her hair rougher than I mean to.

I can feel her smile against my skin, and she looks up at me with a wicked little grin. "I love it when you lose control," she says.

"I love that you do this to me," I reply, my voice low and strained. "No woman has ever even touched me there before. I had no idea I liked it. "

"Good," she says, pulling away with a grin. "Because I like being the first. I plan on doing it a lot more."

Her words make my cock throb. "I'm not going to be able to take much of that, sweetheart."

"That's too bad," she says, pouting. "I'm really enjoying it."

"You're a little tease, Cherry."

"I just want to make you feel good, Max." She diverts my attention, teasing me some more. "I love your tattoos," she says, tracing the most intricate design with her tongue.

Then she fucking latches on to my nipple again, surprising the fuck out of me. I suck in a breath of too much air until she lets go.

"Did you like that?" she whispers, her breath hot on my skin.

"Yes," I hiss out, feeling the electricity run through me.

Cherry continues to tongue my nipples, slowly adding more pressure then backing off, then sucking them again until I'm sure I'm going to come right then and there. Then she pinches one hard in her fingers while sucking the other. I feel it like a direct jolt to my cock, and I groan loudly.

Precum is soaking my boxer briefs. I'm never going to make it through this night. I walk her backwards and toss her on the bed, following so she's pinned beneath me, her wrists cuffed in my hand above her head, my chest making skin-to-skin contact with hers.

I lean down and take her nipple in my mouth, sucking hard while I pinch the other. She cries out and arches her back, wanting more.

"Like that?"

"Yes," she hisses. She's so responsive that I can barely control myself.

"I want to hear you say it," I growl.

"More. Please."

"That's a good girl."

I continue on her other nipple, biting and licking her until her hips are writhing against mine. I let go of her hands and my hands find their way to her hips, gripping her firmly as I nuzzle her skin, getting closer and closer to her center. I let my breath wash over her skin, feeling the little shivers that ripple through her body as I get nearer.

"I can't wait to taste you. Your pussy is going to taste so fucking sweet."

"Please, Max."

Another growl rumbles up my throat.

"Please what? Say it."

"Please, I want your mouth on me," she begs.

I grab her thighs and part them, giving myself more access to her heat. My breath is hot on her pussy and her hips buck up.

"You want my mouth on you, sweetheart?"

"Yes, oh God, yes," she moans.

I breathe in her scent and my cock strains against my jeans for release. I want to be inside of her so badly. I want to feel her wet and tight as I fuck her senseless. I want her to scream my name.

I move my hand between her thighs and brush my thumb across her clit and she moans loudly.

"You're fucking soaked, Cherry. You want me to tongue fuck this little pussy?"

"God, yes!"

"You want me to lick you until you come all over my face?"

"Yes, Max. I want everything with you."

I kiss the inside of her thighs and then lay my tongue flat on her pussy and lick her. She tastes better than anything I've ever had in my mouth.

My tongue laps at her clit and she cries out, her hips bucking up, pushing her against my mouth. I open her up with my fingers and my tongue is inside her. I fuck her with it until she's crying my name and writhing against me. I have to hold her hips down so she doesn't buck us both off the bed.

"I'm going to make you come, Cherry. I'm going to feel you come all over my face."

"Yes, yes."

I lower my head between her legs again and start to lap at her hungrily. My tongue circles her clit, teasing and flicking it while my fingers find their way inside her. She writhes beneath me and I can feel her orgasm building, her breathing becoming increasingly rapid.

"Oh my God, Max," she moans.

I back off a little until she's writhing against me, begging me to keep going. When I flick my tongue over her clit again, she cries out, her body tightens, and she comes all over my face. I lap up every drop as she cries out, her body trembling as her orgasm courses through her. I continue to lap at her gently, slowing as she comes down from her high. I lay my head on her mound and just breathe her in.

"You taste fucking amazing," I whisper as I kiss her thigh.

I kiss my way up her body and she opens her eyes, a smile on her lips. She looks like a well-loved woman.

"I need you inside me, Max."

"No."

Twelve

Cherry

*N*o? Did he just say *no*?

"Why not?" Why won't he fuck me?

Max rolls me to my side so he can spoon me from behind. The denim of his jeans is rough on my naked body, but not in a bad way.

"I told you we're taking it slow."

Slow? "You just...I'm naked ...and you had your mouth on me. This isn't slow. This is the opposite of slow."

Max sniffs my hair, nuzzling deep into my neck. "Cherry, are you begging me to fuck you?"

"Yes!"

He chuckles. "Not tonight."

I groan and am grateful that he can't see me pouting. He soothes me with smooth, long strokes down my arm and sides.

"Max?"

"Hmmm?"

"Doesn't it hurt? For guys when they get worked up and don't..."

"You don't have to worry about that, sweetheart. I'll live, I promise."

If I didn't feel his hard cock pushing into me, I might worry that maybe I wasn't affecting him as much as he was affecting me.

"I want to please you, too," I say, my voice giving away my insecurity, I'm sure.

"Eating your pussy pleased me very much."

My mind goes into overtime trying to figure out what else I can do to convince him. Max rubs his hand up and down my arm, and I know he's trying to relax me.

It's totally not working.

"I don't need you to do anything else. I'm satisfied just being here with you."

"That sounds like something they say in cheesy just say no movies about teen sex. I expect more out of the town bad boy. You have a reputation, Max. You rode into town on a motorcycle to take on the corrupt mayor. You're supposed to be a reckless Romeo. Why won't you fuck me?"

Max laughs. "You're such a greedy girl."

I think for a minute. "Max...at least let me see it."

"Cherry," his tone is a warning.

I roll over, our faces close. "I have needs, Max."

He arches a brow. "Really? Tell me about these needs of yours." He takes one of my fingers into his mouth and sucks it gently. Which is distracting. But he's waiting for me to answer him about my sexual needs. Which is hard for me to talk about. But I can use this to my advantage and maybe get him so horny he'll have no choice but to plow me into the mattress.

Be brave, girl.

"I think about your cock a lot, Max. Wondering what it looks like. How it would feel on my tongue. In my mouth."

His breathing changes, and he takes my finger out of his mouth. "Tell me more, naughty girl. Tell me what you need."

"I imagine how you'll taste. I think about you fucking my mouth."

He squeezes my hand. Kinda hard. "Fuck, Cherry."

"I'll sink to my knees for you, pull your cock out of your jeans and open my mouth." I lick my lips, remembering one of my recent fantasies.

"Cherry, you should stop talking." His voice is stretched thin.

"I want to taste you, Max. I want you to fuck my mouth until you come."

He growls, sliding his hand over my body. "You play dirty."

I think I've got him now.

"Of course, I don't know what I'm doing so you'll have to help me. You'll have to show me how to please you." I blink as prettily as I can manage. "Will you teach me how to suck your cock, Max?"

"Fuck." He rolls out of bed and comes around to my side, pulling me up to sitting at the edge. He looks positively feral. I did this to him. Me.

"So naughty girl thinks she's ready to suck cock, does she?" He undoes the buttons of his jeans. "Show me, then."

I've certainly read enough blow job scenes in my books that I have a good idea what happens. But that bulge seems impossibly big.

My hand is shaking as I reach for him. I can't believe it. I'm about to see it.

I pull his pants down, his briefs coming with them. His giant cock bounces up, hitting his stomach.

God, it's huge!

Okay, it's okay. I can totally do this.

It's enormous, veiny, and hard. I'm mesmerized. I can't take my eyes off it as he steps out of his pants and kicks them away.

"Get on your knees, Cherry."

"Yes." It comes out like a whisper. I'm so excited, I can barely think straight.

His cock is right in front of me. I lean in and inhale his scent at the base. His musky scent makes me wet. I lick the tip, tasting him. Salty. Salty and delicious.

His moan of pleasure vibrates through my body, and I can feel my own desire rising. I'd hoped I would like how it tastes, but admit I was a little worried that I'd feel prudish about the whole thing.

I feel the opposite of prudish right now.

I wrap my fingers around the base, stroking lightly toward the head. He closes his eyes. I lick him from root to tip. He's so hot in my hand. I can't wait to have him in my mouth.

Max gasps as I slip the tip of his cock into my mouth. My pussy clenches, wishing to be filled. My whole body is vibrating in anticipation. I swirl my tongue around him, then back to the tip.

"You look so pretty down there, sweetheart. I love the way you're looking at my cock." He cups the back of my head, his fingers grasping my hair as I focus on exploring every inch of him.

I go faster, licking and sucking and swirling my tongue around the head. He's breathing heavier now, and I can tell I'm making him feel good. I start to feel more confident and I go harder, taking more of him into my mouth with each stroke. He puts one hand on my head, pushing me down. I take him deeper, letting him guide me.

"Fuck. Sweetheart, I can't take much more." He's moaning louder now, and his cock twitching in my mouth. I know he's close. I quicken my pace, feeling his shaft swell even more.

"Do you want my cum, sweetheart? Do you want me to come in your naughty mouth?"

"Mmm-hmm," I say.

"Fuck. Say mmmm again. That feels incredible."

"Mmmmmm," I repeat.

"Your mouth is perfect."

His body starts to tremble, and I know he's about to come. I hope I like this part as much as I like the first part.

His breathing is ragged now, and his fingers are gripping my hair tightly as he thrusts into me with one last, hard push. He lets out a loud groan as he releases a hot stream of cum into my mouth.

It slides down my throat as I swallow greedily, but not expertly by any means, savoring every drop but also making a mess. His orgasm is long and deep, seemingly endless.

I can't keep up with the volume, and I choke a little, but I keep going, determined to take every last drop.

Finally, he pulls out, spent. I can feel the cum dripping down my chin as I look up at him.

"I'm in fucking awe of you, sweetheart. That was amazing." He presses his thumb onto my face, catching the trail that dribbled out and pushing it back toward my mouth.

I part my lips and he slides his thumb into my mouth. I suck on it and he groans. "I'm getting hard again. Fuck if that isn't the hottest damn thing. You're perfect."

"So now will you fuck me?" I ask, because my pussy is clenching around the void and I want him so badly.

"No," he answers.

Again.

I open my mouth to protest his aggravating answer of no, *again*, but then Max tells me, "You're so fucking perfect baby."

He slides us up to the pillows and collapses on top of me, his weight a welcome pressure. His hands caress my skin tenderly, his lips searching for mine.

"I'm going to knock you up someday soon," he whispers in my ear, his breath hot against my skin.

I gasp at his words, feeling a sudden wave of pleasure and heat wash over me. I'm filled with anticipation and excitement as I imagine being impregnated by him.

His hard cock presses against my inner thighs, and I can feel the want radiating from his body and into mine.

He's hard again. He just spent a *lot* of cum, but he's hard again. How is that possible?

Max gently runs his fingers down my body and whispers again, telling me how he wants to fill me up with his seed and make a baby with me.

I arch into him, wanting nothing more than to be filled by him. Now we are getting somewhere. "Yes," I moan. "Please."

He pulls back, nipping my lips before he speaks. "Not tonight."

"Max–"

"I won't take your virginity tonight, sweetheart," he growls as his hands trace my body. I shiver in pleasure under his touch. "But I need to feel you against me now." His voice is demanding and possessive, his words melting over my skin like honey.

"We don't have to wait," I complain. "Please, I need you inside me."

He shakes his head and settles between my legs, guiding his cock and spreading my wetness over the tip. I feel his hard length pressing against me, preparing to enter. "Just a little taste," he says.

I feel my heart start to race. I'm ready. I know I'm ready. I'm more than ready. I can't wait. I'm so ready that I wrap my legs around him and start to pull him close. The head of his cock is pressing against my entrance, teasing me and making me want him more. I moan, desperate to feel him inside me.

He takes my hands in his and pulls me closer, his hips starting to move, easing just the tip into me, just a little bit. It's such sweet torture, and I can't help but arch against him, wanting more. He stops and pulls out, his eyes heavy with lust.

"Not tonight, sweetheart."

"Please," I sob. "I need you."

"Such a greedy, naughty girl."

He's still holding my hands, so I can't move. He keeps his hips pressed against mine, grinding against me until I'm completely lost.

His movements are teasing and sensual, edging me toward orgasm. His thrusts become more urgent, grinding against my clit, and my orgasm gathers just behind my navel. Every nerve in my body is on fire. I'm going to burst out of my skin.

As much as I'm desperate for him to take me all the way, this slow build is driving me wild with desire. I like it but I hate it.

"Please," I whimper, not even knowing what I'm asking for. He's intent on teasing us both until we just die, I guess.

"Please, what? "

"I need you inside me." I can barely form words, my entire body filled with a desperate need for him to fill me. "Please."

"Not yet," he teases.

He shifts his hips so the head of his cock presses against my entrance again. He holds me there, not allowing me to move.

"Please," I whimper, my voice shaking. I'm sweating with need. "Please."

"God, you're so beautiful when you beg, sweetheart. I love seeing you like this." His words are low, sending heat through my body. He slides the tip out again and I sob. "This is killing me too. You're so hot and wet. I want to fuck you so bad."

"Then do it. Fuck me. Put a baby in me. Do it," I challenge.

His face turns to stony determination, the tendons in his neck standing out. "Minx." He pulls my hands up above my head and pins me down with his hips, grinding against me until I'm whimpering his name. "Come for me, my little horny angel," he whispers. "Come against my cock."

His words are like gas on a bonfire. The first wave radiates through me, my heart racing and my body trembling with ecstasy.

He continues to thrust against my clit until I'm lost in a sea of pleasure, but the waves have no end and no beginning. Just a continuous surge of delight.

When I finally come back from my journey, he is still pressed hard against me and his cock twitching, hard.

"I want you to come for me too," I whisper.

He starts to rock again, the movement intensifying and sending me back over the edge. He stops, his muscles straining, and he yells his release. His hot seed spills out all over my pussy. He covers me in it.

He pulls away, dripping with come and I reach down, letting it pool on my fingers. I love the feel of it, so thick and hot. I bring my fingers to my mouth, tasting his cum as I moan with pleasure.

It's like a drug to me, a sweet and salty addiction that drives me wild. He watches hungrily as I lick my fingers.

"Fuck, you're so sexy," he groans. His arms wrap around me and he pulls me up to his chest, resting my head on his shoulder. His scent is strong and male, the sweet smell of the woods and rain and sweat. "You're like this fucking unicorn of a woman. Shy and sweet one minute, and earthy as fuck the next."

"Earthy as fuck, huh?" I ask drowsily.

"Cherry, watching you enjoy my jizz has been the highlight of my life. You're like addicted to it."

I laugh softly. "I think that's a fair description."

He chuckles and I can feel his chest shake. "I'm in over my head with you. You know that, right?"

"I think I'm starting to," I murmur.

"Good." He presses a soft kiss to my forehead and I sigh contentedly.

"It's nice to feel wanted."

He pulls away and meets my gaze with a smoldering look. "You are wanted, sweetheart. Very much."

"When are we going to fuck, though?"

"Not tonight, Cherry. Not tonight."

Thirteen

Max

On Monday, I meet Adam at school, previously arranging with Cherry to pick him up.

"What's going on," he asks me suspiciously.

"I want you to meet someone," I say, as we turn onto the road that leads us just to the outskirts of town.

"The artist?" he asks, thrumming in his seat. "You weren't shitting me about that?"

"Does Cherry let you talk like that?" I ask in the most authoritative voice I can.

"No," he says sheepishly.

"I guess we won't tell her then."

That earns me at least one point with the middle schooler, judging by the smile he's trying not to let happen. "And yes. Just like I promised, I am going to introduce you to my friend Ahmed. He's going to take you under his wing for the mural project at the auto shop unless you fuck up."

"I'll be good. I promise."

We get to Dillon's shop. Right now, he's doing all the mechanic shit himself. Once we get further into fixing the town of Tempest, he's going to hire mechanics for the repair shop and build another bay so he can get back into the custom work that made him so much more money in LA.

And that will bring in some nice rich tourist money for the town. The people that hire Dillon have a lot of cash, and they like to part with it in ways that make them look extravagant.

We get out of the truck, and I steer Adam with a hand on his shoulder into the shop. The kid needs more positive male role models. His dad might get his shit together in rehab this time, but Adam hasn't had his dad's full attention for most of his life.

My brothers and I grew up without a dad, and while our mom did her best, it's hard to figure out a lot of man shit on your own. We turned out okay, after a lot of too-wild years, but maybe we can help Adam so he doesn't struggle like we did.

And help Cherry in the process.

I'll do whatever I can to make her life easier. She's too young to have mostly raised her kid brother on her own. And I recognize a lot of myself in Adam. He could get into a lot of trouble if left to his own devices.

I know I did.

We enter the shop and Ahmed and Dillon are shooting the shit. I introduce Adam to them both and Ahmed takes Adam outside to show him his vision for the building. We talked earlier, and my brothers and I are excited by his idea for the murals. He's covering the building in color inspired by modern tattoo sleeves.

William and I discuss some business while we wait. We're trying to get our chocolatier friend to open a shop downtown. It's not an easy sell. Not yet. The town of Tempest probably can't support a chocolate shop. Not until we can get tourism to return. But the only way to do that is getting businesses like gourmet chocolate shops to open. We need to draw both the tourists and the businesses. But it's a chicken and egg riddle.

"Isn't Jan's wife a school administrator?" Dillon asks.

"Yeah, last I heard. Why?"

"The school principal brought his car in this morning. He just got offered a job in Ohio. His folks live there, so he's going to take it."

Fuck. We can't afford to lose...oh. "Jan's wife probably gets a lot more money in California. Tempest only has one school and piss poor budget if it's anything like the rest of town."

"Yeah," Dillon says, "but if you're wanting to start a family, small town is the way to go. At least, that's what I'd tell a young couple like Jan and Ashley."

He's absolutely right.

"I'll call Jan later. That's fucking genius."

Dillon shrugs. "I have my moments. What's going on with Cherry? If you're bringing her brother into this, I hope you're still serious."

"I'm not bringing Adam into anything just so I can fuck his sister if that is what you're asking me. You know me better than that. You just want me to say some sappy shit so you can make fun of me."

He waits.

I rake my hand through my hair. "I'm fucking in love with her. I'm trying to convince her that we should get married and move into Mom's house."

Dillon whistles through his teeth. "Keep in mind you've known her for what...four days?"

"When you know, you know."

He shakes his head. "You told me you were never going to get married. She's young. She's probably going to want kids. You don't want–"

"I'll take as many kids as I can plant in that woman. I'm fucking gone, Dillon."

That shocks him stupid, so I head out to find Adam and Ahmed. When I bring the kid to Cherry at the bookstore after we're done, he doesn't shut up for long enough to take a breath. She looks at me stunned.

"Adam," she says, "that sounds great. Um, do you have homework?"

He loses his spark and heads into the back room to finish his math.

Cherry smiles at me. It's like being hit with a spotlight of sunshine. "Thank you so much for doing this for him. He's so excited about helping Ahmed. I don't think he uses that many words in a normal day. I can't remember the last time he willingly shared with me what was going on in his life."

"Teenage boys are tricky," I agree. When I'm sure he's out of sight, I grab Cherry and kiss her long and deep. "I missed you."

She laughs against my lips. "It's been a few hours."

"Feels like a lifetime." I kiss her again. "What have you been up to this afternoon?"

"Figuring out the software. And look," she points to a shelf with about five books on it, "our first box came! I entered them into inventory, which was easy because they are all the same title, but it feels real now."

The sheer joy on her face makes me so happy. I wrap my arms around her and kiss her forehead. "You're doing an amazing job, Cherry."

She grins. "Thanks. I'm still learning, but I'm really enjoying it. I never knew I could be so passionate about inventory control."

"What else are you passionate about?" I slide my hand up her waist to cup one of her luscious tits.

"Oh, you know," she says, batting her lashes. "Books, music, lemon meringue, the taste of your cock."

I groan. "You're going to be the death of me, woman."

The door jingles and we turn toward it.

Fucking Chad Hamilton.

"I'm here to check on your permits," he says.

Cherry and I roll our eyes.

"Everything is in order," I say, not bothering to hide my annoyance.

"Good to know," he says, not bothering to look around. He's staring right at Cherry. Her tits mostly. "I'd like to see what you've got."

I want to kill him, but I can't because prison isn't in my five-year-plan. I just scowl and step in between them.

"We've filed all the necessary permits with the state and county. As you know, the town doesn't actually have a business inspection process, Hamilton. You have no jurisdiction here. If there's nothing else," I say.

"My father is mayor and he asked me to check."

I roll my eyes. "Well, your father is wrong. You have no authority here. Now, if there is nothing else, I'd like you to leave."

"It's a place of business. You can't dictate who comes in."

My hands ball into fists, but Cherry strokes a gentle hand down my back, calming me down. "A place of business is private property, Hamilton. I can serve who I like and not serve who I don't. Besides that, we're not even open yet."

He looks like he's about to argue, but then he turns and leaves without another word.

Cherry lets out a huge sigh of relief. I put my arm around her and pull her close. "You okay?"

She looks up at me with her big gray eyes and nods. "Yeah. I just don't like him. Remember how I was telling you I got teased a lot growing up because of my chest?" She points to her very generous breasts. The breasts I am eager to fuck. "Chad Hamilton was my biggest bully."

My blood boils and I want to go after him. But I know that won't help Cherry. "The way he acts around you, I thought he was trying to get you to go out with him."

"That's a recent development. Most of his friends have moved away, since Tempest is becoming nearly a ghost town. And that means that most single women are gone too. He assumed I'd worship his attention. I didn't."

"He must be pretty pissed that you're with me instead of him."

She sighs. "It's his own fault. He's been an asshole to me, to most women actually, his whole life."

I'll have to keep an eye on that situation. He's not going to just give up. Entitled guys like Chad think they can take what they want.

But she's not alone now. She's got me. She'll have my brothers too, if necessary.

I protect what's mine. He's not getting near her again.

• • • •

IT'S BEEN A BUSY FUCKING week and Friday is finally here. Cherry is dropping her brother off at Mary's, and I am getting the steaks ready.

I don't know how I'm going to keep from fucking her this weekend. I'm twisted up with need. I keep having to remind myself that we've only known each other a week. That I'm trying to make sure she understands that she's it for me, that I love her, before we have sex. I don't want to rush things. I've never been in this kind of relationship before. Rushing things might scare her off.

I plan on eating that sweet pussy as much as possible this weekend, though.

The rain is really coming down now, so maybe I'll have to cook the steaks inside after all. A rumble of thunder sounds. Yeah, probably inside is better.

I look around the house to make sure I didn't leave a mess anywhere. The new furniture is nothing special since I'm planning on waiting for Cherry to pick out what we want when she moves in with me. But I don't want her sitting on the floor in the meantime.

She knocks and I feel a wave of contentment sweep over me. She's here. I always feel better when I'm with her.

I open the door. "You don't have to knock. I gave you a key."

She steps in. "It's not polite just to barge into someone's house."

I don't want to argue with her. "Let me take your raincoat."

Cherry undoes the belt and slowly lets the coat open and slide down her shoulders. My heart stops. My breath catches. My dick nearly breaks my zipper.

Underneath that long coat, Cherry is dressed only in little scraps of black lace.

The lingerie clings to her curves, showing off her ample tits and round ass. She's wearing black thigh-high stockings with lace tops, the black contrasting with the milky white of her thighs.

She hands me the coat and shakes out her long sable brown hair. "It's really coming down out there."

My tongue is stuck to the roof of my mouth. I can't think of anything to say.

Cherry notices my stunned expression and gives me a slow, sexy smile. "I thought you might like it."

My brain finally kicks back in. "You look amazing."

The wind picks up outside and the power flickers.

I can't think of another thing to say, so I pick her up fireman style and head to the bedroom.

"Max!"

The smack I give her on her bottom quiets her for a second. "You knew exactly what was going to happen to you when you showed up at my door wearing that." I spank her again. "You'll do anything to get my fat cock in your pussy won't you?"

I toss her on the bed.

"Yes," she moans. "Yes, I will."

Her answer sends a thrill through my body. I'm so fucking lucky to have her. I'd do anything for her.

But for now, all I want is to make her scream my name. I look my fill at those curves and the minx spreads her legs open, showing me the lingerie is crotchless.

"You're such a naughty girl. Look at that pussy, so wet and ready for me."

I grab her hands and pin them above her head. She can't move. I'm in control. My cock is rock hard and I can't wait to slip it inside her tight heat.

"You want me to fuck you tonight? Be sure, sweetheart, once I get inside your tight pussy, I won't pull out. Not until I fill you up with all my come."

She nods and moans. "Yes, please. Fill me up."

I dip my head and start licking and sucking, avoiding her clit until she's panting and moaning my name. I'm not going to last much longer.

"I love the way you taste, such a sweet hot pussy." My hands undo my jeans, freeing my raging hard on. The relief is short lived. I need inside her.

Shucking my clothes, I position myself above her, nudging her open with my cock, using her sweet pussy cream to lubricate. "I don't want to hurt you, sweetheart. It's your first time."

With one thumb on her clit, I slide my cock in, inch by inch, pausing as she acclimates until I'm buried balls deep. She's tighter than tight, but I didn't feel a hymen in our way, so at least it didn't hurt as much as I thought it might.

"Oh God, you feel so good, sweetheart." I have to use every muscle in my body to hold still and allow her to accommodate my cock. "You doing okay?"

"Yes, I'm better than I've ever been in my whole life."

I take it slow, savoring every second. She moans and writhes beneath me. I increase my pace, my thrusts getting harder, faster. Less controlled. She wraps her legs around my waist and holds me tight as I thrust into her over and over. Her tits jiggle in that black lace like a dream.

Her orgasm builds and she cries out my name as I drive myself deep into her. Her tight walls start milking my cock, and I'm gone. It's too intense. Cherry's pussy is like a religious experience.

She comes hard, screaming my name, and I lose any control I had. I'm going to fill her up. I'm one step removed from an animal.

She's getting all of me, and I come harder than I ever have before.

My cock is twitching and pulsing inside her, shooting my cum deep into her womb. I collapse onto her, burying my face in the crook of her neck while my cock keeps twitching, leaking into her.

We lay there panting and sweaty, my cum dripping out of her onto the bed sheets.

I'd do anything for this woman. I'd die for her. I love her so much.

"I'm never letting you go, Cherry."

She strokes her hand through my hair, down my back. "As if I would let you."

I pull out and we both groan. I run my hand over her stomach. I love the feel of her soft flesh. The roundness of her tummy, the shape of her hips. "I'm going to fuck you ten times a day until this has our baby in it."

"That sounds like a full time job. How are we going to save Tempest if all we ever do is have sex?"

I kiss her navel. "Fine. Five times a day."

"Three and it's a deal."

I raise my head to look at her. She's well pleased with a softness that makes me fall harder. I did that. I took her worries and made her look like that.

"I'm serious. I have a new breeding fetish, woman." I palm a breast and imagine it even bigger and filled with milk. "Did you renew that subscription to the bridal magazine yet?"

"You're crazy."

She doesn't know the half of it.

She holds my hand to her stomach and gets quiet. "I know all the things I should do. All the reasonable and logical things because getting pregnant seems unreasonable and illogical for us right now. But Max, the idea of it..."

"Me, too, Cherry."

We catch each other's gazes. Her breath shudders out of her like she's been holding it. "I want to have a baby with you."

"I want that, too."

"But–"

I kiss the protest off her lips. "We'll make it work. I promise."

I scoop her into my arms and kiss her until we both forget the world around us. Nothing else matters but us. She's mine, and I'm never letting her go.

Epilogue

Cherry

Three months later

The phone rings. "Tempest Books," I answer.

"Cherry?"

My heart drops. "Dad? Is everything okay?"

He clears his throat. "Yeah, sorry. Didn't mean to scare you. I have an appointment with the VA next Wednesday, and I wanted to see if Adam could hang out with you after school. Maybe you could feed him dinner too? It's an afternoon appointment, and it's in the city so I won't be home until later."

Whew.

"Sure. Is Mary taking you or do you need a ride?"

"Mary is driving."

I had kind of assumed since they have been doing an awful lot together. Enough so that he got a new sponsor since she didn't want to cross any lines.

It's a little weird. My dad and my old boss. But they are saying they are just good friends. At least until he's been sober for a year. But I've been learning that as far as Dad goes, we don't think about next year. We go one day at a time.

My dad and Adam moved into Max's bungalow. Max and I are living in his childhood home and fixing it up together in the evenings.

My childhood home is being gutted in a different phase of our Tempest plan, so it's sitting empty now. It can sit empty forever. I don't want to see it again.

I had given up hope of ever being able to move out of that house, thinking I was trapped. Adam would grow up, sure, but my dad wasn't showing signs of ever being able to manage himself. But after some long talks with Mary, I realized that I have to stop being codependent. She helped me find a counselor, too. Now Max and I are the backup plan for Adam. I'm no longer the sole caregiver. If Dad starts drinking again, Adam will move in with us. But my dad is not my responsibility.

I hang up the phone and lock the door. Closing time.

The bookstore is a dream come true. We worked so hard to make it perfect. The shop is cozy, packed full of books from floor to ceiling. Yes, the ceiling. Because I really wanted a rolling ladder like Belle. Yes, when no one is here, I do my best impression. Why wouldn't I?

I walk to the back of the store and turn off the lights, leaving only a few lamps on to illuminate the cozy reading nooks we've created.

I hear the backdoor and recognize Max's footsteps. The familiar flutter in my belly starts up, and I turn to see him walking towards me, his eyes fixed on mine.

"Hey," he says, wrapping his arms around me and pulling me close. "How was your day?"

"Good," I reply, snuggling into his embrace. "Busy, but good. What about yours?"

He shrugs. "Better now." He inhales my scent deeply. "Much better now. Oh, hey, I heard some interesting gossip today."

"Max, you're spending way too much time at the lunch counter. You're beginning to sound like them."

"I'm winning over the old cronies, aren't I? Coffee at the diner every morning has done more for my image than any donations to the Kiwanis have." He doesn't wait for my response. "The mayor's daughter got kicked out of her university."

Since it's barely into September, that's quite an achievement. "Cressida Hamilton is a spoiled brat, from what I remember. Not a bully like her brother, but not an easy girl to be around. Did they say why she got expelled?"

Max double-checks all the doors. "Nah. I heard all kinds of speculation, but nobody knows. Also, Mayor Hamilton has a new lawyer. The man never leaves his side. They are up to something."

I grab my purse and phone. "It's really weird to me that Mayor Hamilton is still fighting us so hard. Most people in town are happy with the changes so far. It's like he has a vested interest in the town completely dying." I pause. "You don't think that's it, do you? Does he want Tempest to fail? How would that benefit him? If there was some financial reason behind that, then no wonder he's so mad your company bought all the empty shops."

Max takes my hand and we exit out the back. "I think maybe it's time we hire a private investigator. We should look into this lawyer too. You're getting my spidey senses tingling."

"When we get home, you can tingle some of my senses if you want."

"Maybe I'll tingle some of them in the car on the way home."

He does. When he parks in front of the house, he's still got his hand up my dress and his fingers in my panties and I'm coming again.

"Can you walk, sweetheart?"

"Probably not, but I'll try."

When we walk into the house, my heart feels full. It's a big old farmhouse, too big for the two of us. Someday, we will fill it with kids.

We practice making babies as often as possible.

We walk down the hall to get to the living room, I'm looking forward to a glass of wine and maybe a small fire. It's not really cold enough for a fire yet, but it sounds cozy. In just a few months, my life has changed so much. I love going to work for a change, but even better, I love coming home.

I stop. The living room is overflowing with bright, cheerful blooms of all different kinds of flowers. Red roses, yellow daisies, blue hydrangeas–and all shapes and sizes of balloons, bobbing against the ceiling. A soft, sweet-smelling fragrance drifts through the air, and the sunlight that streams through the window is glinting off of the vibrant colors of the bouquets.

I turn to Max. "What?"

He's on his knee. Holding a ring.

I gasp. "You are not."

"Yes I am. I love you. Marry me."

"Max!"

I can't believe it. This is the moment I've been waiting for my whole life, practicing for since I was a girl, and I knew it was coming. And yet it still catches me off guard. I stare at the ring in his hand, the diamond sparkling in the dim light of the living room. This is it. This is the man I want to spend the rest of my life with. My childhood dream coming true.

He clears his throat. "That wasn't a yes, sweetheart. Want to try again?"

"Yes. Yes yes yes yes yes."

And then, I'm in his arms.

"Does this mean Edward and Jacob are finally off the menu?"

I smile recalling my childhood weddings to them too. "Nothing wrong with a little healthy competition, Mr. Duke."

He chuckles and then tickles me, making me squeal with laughter before bending me over the couch and lifting my skirt. I can feel his breath on my neck as he whispers in my ear, "You ready to make this official?"

I nod eagerly.

Max holds up my hand behind me and slides the ring onto my finger and then kisses the back of my neck tenderly.

"Welcome to forever, sweetheart."

I try to pull my hand down to look at the ring, but he doesn't let go, instead grabbing both my wrists behind me, trapping me. I hear the unzipping of his jeans.

"Max?"

His hard cock presses against my ass and he grunts. I'm pinned in place.

My panties are pushed to the side. I'm still soaked from the orgasms in the car.

"No more waiting," he says, sliding through my slick folds.

And then, he plunges himself inside me.

"This is how it's going to be, sweetheart," he growls. "Forever."

My heart races as I let him take me, and I know I never want to be without him again.

This is what I was meant for. This is forever.

I'm so full of him as he rocks into me, and I can't help but cry out in pleasure. "You're so big, Max. I'm so full."

Just a few months ago I was lonely. My self-esteem was garbage. And I had nothing to look forward to.

Now my life is completely different. I have someone to love, somebody who loves me back. I have a future and a happily ever after. And a huge cock that never seems to get tired of pleasing me.

"That's it, baby. Clench around my cock. Make it official."

I moan as I do as he says, and he pushes me over the edge.

"You're milking my cock, sweetheart. Gonna make me fill you up."

"Put your baby in me, Max. I'm ovulating."

Max groans, collapsing on top of me as he fills me deeply.

We lay there for a few moments, neither of us wanting to move. Finally, I turn my head so I can look up at him.

"Forever," I whisper.

Max smiles and leans down to kiss me. "Forever."

• • • •

Do you like free books? Exclusive content? Bonus material? Join my mailing list and never miss a new release or news from Brill Harper. Get your free story called CODE OF LOVE here: https://dl.bookfunnel.com/abimfytcoo

Also by Brill Harper

Blue Collar Bad Boys
Bounced
Nailed: A Blue Collar Bad Boys Book
Drilled: A Blue Collar Bad Boys Book
Wrecked: A Blue Collar Bad Boys Book
Laid: A Blue Collar Bad Boys Book
Tagged
Plowed
Bucked: A Blue Collar Bad Boys Book
Banged: A Blue Collar Bad Boys Book
Tapped: A Blue Collar Bad Boy Book

Dukes of Tempest
Mad Max
Dirty Dillon: A Small Town Age Gap Romance

It's Complicated
All Together

All at Once

Love in Brazen Bay
Wrong Number Text
The Right Stuff
So Wrong It's Right
Don't Get Me Wrong

Standalone
Dirty Jobs: a Blue Collar Bad Boys Collection
Notch on His Bedpost
Honeymoon With The Prince: A Royal Romance
Good Girl

Watch for more at https://brillharper.com.

About the Author

Unfailingly filthy...and super sweet

Brill's books are filthy/sweet for when you're in the mood for something a little over the top. Okay, a lot over the top. Sorry, not sorry. Members of the Brilliance Club get early access to all Brill's work and exclusive content not available anywhere else.

Find out more: **https://reamstories.com/brillharper**

Brill Harper is represented by Deidre Knight of The Knight Agency.

Read more at https://brillharper.com.